The Golden Spur

OTHER SAGEBRUSH LARGE PRINT WESTERNS BY
WALKER A. TOMPKINS

Border Ambush

Flaming Canyon

The Golden Spur

WALKER A. TOMPKINS

Library of Congress Cataloging in Publication Data

Tompkins, Walker A.
The golden spur / Walker A. Tompkins.
p. cm. (large print)
Originally published: London : Robert Hale, 1995, in series: A black horse western.
ISBN 1-57490-253-9 (alk. paper)
1. Large type books. I. Title.

PS3539.03897 G66 2000
813'.54—dc21 99-053222

Cataloguing in Publication Data is available from the British Library and the National Library of Australia.

Sagebrush Large Print Westerns are published in the United States and Canada by Thomas T. Beeler, Publisher, Box 659, Hampton Falls, New Hampshire 03844-0659. ISBN 1-57490-253-9

Published in the United Kingdom, Eire, and the Republic of South Africa by Isis Publishing Ltd, 7 Centremead, Osney Mead, Oxford OX2 0ES England. ISBN 0-7531-6251-2

Published in Australia and New Zealand by Bolinda Publishing Pty Ltd, 17 Mohr Street, Tullamarine, Victoria, 3043, Australia. ISBN 1-74030-020-3

Manufactured by Sheridan Books in Chelsea, Michigan

CHAPTER 1

Mistaken Identity

OUT OF THE FLAMING TEXAS SUNSET HE CAME, A HARD, bone-lean rider, as ruggedly handsome as the flaxen-tailed palomino he forked; seated loosely in a saddle whose stirrup leathers had been extended to the bottom notch to accommodate his rangy, pony-warped legs.

Ahead of him, lamplight was twinkling in windows along Mexitex's main street, and reflecting in the sluggish waters of the Rio Grande from the Mexican village on the Chihuahua bank. Clay Raine had never drifted up this trail before, and he contemplated a night's stop-over here only because of the coincidence of nightfall and a handy settlement.

For a total stranger, then, it was singular that Raine's arrival seemed to be expected by several persons in Mexitex, though he had told no one of his route between El Paso and Laredo.

Yet, riding in, he was under the keen scrutiny of four pairs of eyes. They were the eyes of the knot of Mexicans grouped in the dingy alley alongside the Longhorn Saloon, and those of a girl who had kept a long, solitary vigil from the porch swing of the Trail House, which was across the street. They seemed to be expecting Clay Raine.

Squinting against the blood-red glare of the western sky where sunset was slowly burning itself out, the girl's lips parted in thanksgiving and relief as she saw Clay Raine halt his leggy palomino in front of the Trail House livery stable, and glance quizzically about.

Leaving the deep cushions of the porch swing, she descended the hotel steps, stifling a desire to call out to the trail-dusty horseman as he swung out of stirrups, trailing rawhide reins through rope-calloused palms.

Raine was crowding thirty, but the crisp russet beard which matted his jaw, plus the harsh lines of fatigue from sixteen hours in the saddle, gave him the appearance of a man of fifty. Pushed back from his alkali-powdered forehead was a flat-crowned Californian sombrero. His wedge-shaped torso was clad in a hickory shirt and calf-hide vest, and he wore the cactus-scuffed bullhide chaps and spurred Coffeyville boots of a range rider.

These details of garb branded him as a roving cowpuncher, and seemed to give the girl momentary doubt. But when the rider turned toward the livery barn entrance, hitching at the weight of double-shell belts and holstered six-guns at either thigh, she saw the initial 'R' worked in tiny brass studs on his batwing chaps.

That initial brushed aside the last vestige of doubt the girl had that this was not the man whose appearance in Mexitex had been the cause of her afternoon's wait on the Trail House porch.

A rustle of buckskin skirts caused Clay Raine to wheel about in time to see the girl rush up to him. A moment later her arms were about his neck, and he felt the pressure of soft, warm lips crowding against his own. He had glimpsed a pair of larkspur eyes and tumbling hair and a curvesome, youthful body.

"Uncle Gid!" she cried, snuggling a tear-moist cheek against his shirt and brushing his jaw with a clustering wealth of chestnut curls. "I—I thought you'd never get here!"

A glint of humor kindled in Raine's granite-gray eyes as he reached up and gently loosened her grip on his neck.

As she moved back, the girl's hair pushed aside the dusty bandanna knotted about the rider's throat, to reveal the badge of a United States deputy marshal pinned to his shirt.

"Oh! I—I'm afraid I mistook you—"

The lawman laughed, a husky laugh due to the alkali grit in his craw.

"Reckon yuh have, ma'am." He chuckled as he saw confusion replace the warm glow in her eyes. "Which same is my tough luck, I reckon. Yuh said somethin' about an uncle—"

The girl broke free of his light touch, embarrassment putting a glow under the bronzed sun-tan of her skin.

"I—please forgive me! I was expecting someone else, someone who rides a palomino like yours. I—"

Wheeling, she fled like a startled rabbit toward the Trail House porch. The screen door slammed on her vanishing figure.

Deputy Marshal Clay Raine stood transfixed, the amusement dying in his eyes as he stared at the hotel door. For a man whose home was the cantle-board of a saddle and whose contact with women was extremely infrequent, the touch of warm feminine lips against his own had been strangely stirring, like the flavor of rare Spanish wine.

"Well!" he grunted, shrugging himself out of revery. "Mexitex's welcomin' committee worked fast, but quit the job too danged sudden. I wonder who in—"

You weesh the *caballo* groomed and grained, senor?"

The slurring voice of a hostler from the Trail House stable cut into Raine's thoughts. He turned to see a serape-clad Mexican youth reaching for his palomino's reins.

"Uh—yeah. Yeah. Treat old Palomar handsome, *hombrecito.* Curry him till he shines like a pickaninny's heel, dish out the best oats yuh got in the barn, and bed down his stall with clean hay. Palomar's pushed back a lot of Texas since mornin'."

"*Si*, senor."

Clay Raine trailed his spurs into the black maw of the livery barn, intending to oversee the hostler's handling of his prime saddler. Once inside the stable doors, he had no way of seeing the three Mexicans who slipped out of the alley from the Longhorn Saloon across the street and headed for the stable like stalking phantoms.

Raine unbuckled his *alforja* bags from behind the cantle and laid them aside. The hostler was hooking a tapaderoed stirrup over the horn, preparatory to unknotting the latigo from its ring, when Raine sensed the presence of three Mexicans converging on him from the barn door.

There was no time for an inkling of peril to communicate itself to the puncher's brain. Lamplight reflected from the saloon windows across the street, glittered on naked gun-metal in the fists of the three Mexicans, two of whom halted at arm's length, with the third just outside the barn door.

"*Maños altos,* senor!" a harsh whisper lashed against Raine's ear-drums. "You weel leeft the hands—"

Raine fell back a step, planting his shoulder blades against the planks of Palomar's stall. Both hands blurred, starting toward the cedar stocks of his low-slung Colts.

But before his hands could reach leather, Clay Raine felt something like a hot needle prick through the fabric of his shirt, low against the ribs on his left side. The livery barn hostler's mescal-fouled breath was hot against the marshal's cheek.

"Make no noise, senor," the stable tender whispered. "Thees *cuchillo* can reach your heart *pronto prontico,* no?"

There was no time to probe into the meaning of the death-trap into which he had stepped. Raine's left hand suddenly lashed down against the hostler's wrist, jerking the long-bladed hunting knife away from his side.

The lawman's elbow came out and up, smashing into the hostler's belly. The stable boy dropped with a grunt of pain. The knife clattered into the straw underfoot as Raine ducked to avoid the down-clubbing revolvers in the hands of the three Mexicans who had followed him into the barn.

Bracing himself against the stall planks, the Texican catapulted outward, his blocky shoulders catching two of the Mexican gunmen knee-high and bowling them to the hoof-packed floor of the barn.

Simultaneously Raine's two .45s leaped from holsters, thumbs earing back knurled gun-hammers for a shoot-out at point-blank range.

A clubbing gun-barrel swiped across Raine's temple, the front sight razoring a slice of flesh from his scalp. He lunged forward on hands and knees, fighting off the blackness which swirled around him, his cow-boots scrambling over the paunch of one of the gunnies he had floored.

A spur rowel lashed out, slicing steel points raking his right arm and paralyzing his hand, allowing the cocked Peacemaker to slide from his grasp.

Dazedly, the Texan reared to his feet and spun about to meet the renewed onslaught of the third Mexican who was lashing desperately at his exposed skull. Before he could lift the gun in his left hand, the two grounded Mexicans had pounced to their feet and flung themselves on him, snarling like cougars.

Against overpowering weight and strength, Clay Raine went down, his free fist hammering at dusky faces in the murk. Twice his rock-hard knuckles landed, and he felt flesh and bone crunch under his punishing blows.

Then a steel-muscled elbow cranked about his throat, strangling him. A hard kick caught him in the solar plexus, numbing his body as if he had been struck by a thunderbolt. He reared to his feet, by sheer force pulling two of his attackers up with him. Lost somewhere underfoot was his second Colt six-gun, and from now on it would be primitive combat against triple odds.

He stopped slugging, to claw at the arm which was threatening to pinch off his windpipe. Spanish oaths crackled in the darkness about him. A haymaker raked his beard, jarred his cheek-bone.

Bleeding, dazed, but struggling with the cold ferocity of a bayed grizzly, Clay Raine went down under the crushing weight of Mexican bodies.

Then a gun-butt clipped him under the ear, and his senses blacked out like a candle flame in a gale.

CHAPTER 2

The Black Wolf

A COOL NIGHT WIND WHIPPING HIS FACE BROUGHT Raine to his senses. He tried to pull a hand up to the throbbing welt on his mastoidal bone. In so doing he made the discovery that his wrists were tied behind his back.

He opened his eyes, tried to cry out. Both efforts were blocked, for a gag had been knotted about his teeth and a blindfold covered his eyes.

As his senses returned, Raine became aware of the fact that he was on horseback. His nostrils, clear of the lower hem of the bandanna which blindfolded him, registered the dank odors of mud and the pungent smell of willows and tule reeds.

Then his ears distinguished sounds—the croaking of bullfrogs, the gurgle of water sluicing over gravelly bars, the splash of horses' hoofs wading through fetlock-deep water.

Water! The Rio Grande river cut off Mexitex from the Mexican town of Coyotero, on the Chihuahua bank. It was the only body of water large enough for a horse to splash through, in these parts. He must be on his way to Coyotero, and from the sounds, several riders were accompanying him.

"I'm being taken across the Rio into Mexico," a thought shot through Clay Raine's pain-numbed brain. "Now why in h—"

Out of the torment of his gun-whipped skull, the Texas deputy believed he knew the answer for his inexplicable attack. These Mexicans must have mistaken him for someone else, just as had the girl who had kissed him the moment of his arrival in Mexitex.

But what lay ahead on the trail he was now traveling, bound and gagged and blindfolded and helpless as a mummy, Raine was too sick and stunned even to wonder about.

He felt the icy contact of water about his boots, and knew from the pitching motion of the horse under him that his captors were swimming the Rio Grande. The saddle he forked was not his own, nor was his mount Palomar, the palomino he had been in the act of stabling at the Trial House barn when he had been attacked. Clay Raine was sure of those two facts, blindfolded though he was. He knew it with the unerring savvy which comes to men born to the saddle.

Emerging from the fog of concussion which had blanked out his sensibilities, Raine tried to sensitize himself to what was going on. He knew by the way he had to fight for balance in the saddle that the horses were leaving the Rio Grande and were slogging up the steep Chihuahua bank.

A few minutes later his captors leveled off on what was probably a trail, and turned left. That conveyed nothing to Raine. His first thought had been that he was on his way to Coyotero, but it might as well be somewhere else. For all he knew, he might have been unconscious for hours, and he might be miles from Mexitex by now.

His captors—he could tell that there were three of them—were probably the Mexicans who had waylaid him in the Mexitex barn. Except for occasional guttural remarks in Spanish, they pushed along the trail with a silence which boded evil to Raine.

The trail dipped downward at a roof-steep angle, and the cowboy lawman became aware of other things. A hum of sound, unintelligible as to detail, connoted the proximity of a settlement of some sort. Yapping dogs; the plaintive bleat of a goat near the trailside; further away, children singing.

At the foot of the trail, the horses' hoofs left the flinty gumbo and began sluffing through dust which rose in stifling clouds to choke Raine's nostrils. He began to sort out individual noises, now—the rattle of crockery dishes in some *jacal,* with attendant odors of *chili colorado* and garlic and *pulque* liquor, emanating from a peon's kitchen along the trail. "We're in a Mex town," he deduced, as the route began making right-angled turns, indicating street intersections. "Since we crossed the Rio, maybe it is Coyotero."

From time to time the breeze was cut off and the blind-folded prisoner sensed walls looming about, from the confined echoes of the mounts' hoofbeats on the hard adobe. Once they skirted a *cantina,* for Raine recognized the chiming of liquor glasses, a senorita's high-pitched peal of laughter, the strumming of a pair of guitars intoning "La Paloma."

Then, abruptly, the horses came to a halt and saddle leather creaked as the Mexican trio of kidnapers dismounted.

Something tugged at Raine's left boot, and he realized that a knife blade was sawing through a rope which had bound his legs together under the pony's belly. Then a rough hand closed about his pinioned elbow and he was assisted to the ground.

Fingers gripped each of his arms, and he was led away from the horses. A key rasped in a lock, and unoiled hinges protested as a door was opened. A dank rush of air, pungent with mingled smells of human sweat and stale tobacco and whisky fumes, met Raine's nostrils.

"Watch the step, Senor Rassmussen. An *escalera*—how the gringo say eet? The stairway."

"Senor Rassmussen!"

Raine's lips twisted in a bitter grin behind his confining gag. First a beautiful girl in cowgirl garb had kissed him and called him "Uncle Gid." Now it was

Senor Rassmussen. What kind of a mix-up had he rammed his horns into, anyway?

His groping feet worked their way down a short flight of steps into what was obviously a cellar. At no time did the pressure of his captors' fingers relax on his forearms, until a second door squeaked open and Raine's eyes detected the faint gleam of a lamp through the bandanna knotted over his brows.

"*Hola,* Senor Black Wolf!" sounded a voice at Raine's left ear, as his captors brought him to a halt on a stone-cobbled floor. "We have the man you weesh to see, *es verdad*!"

A low grunt, dead ahead, greeted the Mexican's announcement. Clay Raine felt something like the cold feet of mice scamper down his backbone, as the name "Black Wolf" rang in his ears.

Here, indeed, was a tangible peril awaiting him at the end of the mystery trail which had had its start in a three-to-one struggle over on the Texas side of the Rio. For the Border outlaw known as the Black Wolf was no stranger to Clay Raine—by name and reputation, at least.

The U.S. Border Patrol, aided by Texas Rangers along the entire length of the Rio Grande, had waged war with the Black Wolf and his legion of Border-hoppers for going on ten years now. Narcotics, aliens, rustled stock, guns and ammunition to outfit Mexican rebels—any and all types of *contrabando* were the Black Wolf's stock in trade.

Glimmerings of the truth began to filter into Clay Raine's mind, as he stood between his Mexican captors and waited for the Black Wolf to speak. The deputy marshal's badge on his shirt was probably going to be his passport to death, this night.

Had news of his trip along the Rio reached the Black Wolf's ears? It seemed logical to assume that this was the explanation of the mysterious attack on him in the Mexitex livery barn. But if so, why had the Black Wolf given orders for his henchmen to kidnap an American lawman, and go through the risky business of smuggling him across the Rio into Mexico? If Raine's death was the Black Wolf's object, a bullet or a blade could have accomplished the job, over in Mexitex.

"If this hombre is Goldpan Rassmussen, the years have changed him more than I thought!" came a throaty voice out of the void. "Take off his blindfold, Esteban."

Fingers fumbled at the bandanna-knot on Raine's neck nape. An instant later the blindfold dropped from his eyes, and the deputy marshal was blinking into the yellow glare of a lamp suspended from a whitewashed ceiling beam.

Raine had a fleeting picture of his surroundings—a cellar beneath a saloon, judging from the huge wine casks and tiered cases of whisky and beer which lined the walls. But the prisoner's gaze was riveted to the smuggler chief standing immediately below the ceiling lamp. The Black Wolf!

Raine saw a lathy man wearing a ball-tassled felt sombrero and a slack broadcloth coat such as those affected by gamblers. He saw the bulge of holstered six-guns thonged against striped breeches which were tucked into polished cowboots.

Then, lifting his slitted orbs to scan the Black Wolf's face, Raine discovered that the notorious outlaw chieftain wore a mask over his entire head—a cornmeal sack, with twin slits cut into the advertising label by way of eye-holes. Under the yellow glare of the overhead lamp, the Black Wolf's mask resembled a grotesque human skull.

There was a moment's steely silence, as the slitted, flint-black eyes behind the Wolf's white mask appraised the Mexicans' prisoner. Then the mask ballooned outward as the Black Wolf gave vent to a snort of disgust.

"You stupid, blundering idiots!" thundered the outlaw, his big hands clenching and opening like an eagle's talons. "This man is not Goldpan Rassmussen! Rassmussen is a man crowding sixty. This hombre you have fetched here is a stripling!"

Raine glanced sideward at Esteban, the Mexican who had untied his blindfold. Esteban's smallpox-pitted moon of a face was leaking sweat now, and the big peon seemed to cringe before the angry eyes of his chief.

"But senor—there ees some mistake!" protested Esteban, rolling his eyes wildly. "Thees hombre, he rode eento Mexitex on a palomino, *si*! And he had the rusty beard such as Senor Rassmussen has, as you yourself told me! By the sacred bones of Santa Gasparo, this man ees—"

The Black Wolf cut off Esteban with an impatient wave of his hand.

"Stop yammering, you *tonto* scum. If this man rode a palomino, it is a coincidence which he has to thank the devil for. But take off his spurs. We shall see."

Clay Raine's brows drew together in a frown of puzzlement, as Esteban's companion stooped and unbuckled his long-shanked Cheyenne spurs. Handing them to the Black Wolf, the Mexican sank to his knees.

"Not only did thees hombre ride a palomino, Senor *Jefe*," he choked out. "When he came to Mexitex, the senorita who is his *sobrina*—how you say, his niece—

she greeted him weeth the kiss, senor! She say, "Oncle Gid, I thought you never come.' I swear it!"

The Black Wolf dropped Raine's spurs onto a barrel-head and reached into his frock coat for a staghorn-butted jack-knife, from the handle of which a pigeon-blood ruby gleamed like a red star in the lamp-shine.

The outlaw seemed to have forgotten the existence of the jabbering Mexicans, as he cleaned off the mud and horsehair which fouled the spur rowels. Carefully he gouged the point of his knife-blade on one of the points of each spur.

"Bah" he snarled, turning to show the Mexicans the result of his examination. "Plain iron spurs! You see the fool's mistake you have made tonight. I don't care if the senorita thought this man was her uncle or not. You have captured the wrong man."

Clay Raine made sputtering sounds behind his gag, as he struggled to free himself of the handkerchief which rendered him mute. A thousand questions clamored within him, but the Black Wolf did not appear to be disposed to have the gag removed.

Tossing the spurs aside, the smuggler chief pocketed his knife and eyed Raine indifferently. Then his body stiffened, as he caught sight of the deputy marshal's star pinned to the waddy's shirt.

"Ah—a John Law!" mused the outlaw. "Esteban and Floriado, you have done a good night's work, for all your blundering stupidity. A *Tejano* lawman is always good game to bag."

Relief was mirrored on the faces of the two Mexicans as they saw the Black Wolf turn his back to them and head toward a stairway which led to an upper room. Reaching the foot of the stairs, the Black Wolf paused as Floriado called out timorously:

"What shall we do weeth this stranger, senor?"

Turning, the Black Wolf laughed harshly behind his mask.

"Take this unlucky John Law up into the Sierra Calientes above the town," ordered the smuggler crisply. "You will dig a grave at the far end of Tequila Canyon, and bury this Texican deep. *Sabe ustedes?* Leave no evidence of a grave behind, for the Mexican *rurale* police to run across. *Adios.*"

With the echoes of the death sentence he had pronounced still resounding in the stuffy cellar, the Black Wolf mounted the stairs and a doorway closed on his towering figure.

CHAPTER 3

"Texan Dig Your Grave!"

FLORIADO WHIPPED A SIX-GUN FROM HOLSTER AS HE saw Clay Raine brace himself, as if to attempt a getaway. Ramming the .45 sight-deep into the deputy marshal's short ribs, Floriado and Esteban shoved their prisoner toward the stairway leading outdoors.

Tangled thoughts raced through Raine's head as he stumbled up the cellar stairway, out into the cool night.

Why had the Black Wolf scratched his knife-blade into the rowels of the spurs? Why had the notorious outlaw been waiting in this underground hide-out for the arrival of the man named Rassmussen, the uncle of a girl whose name Raine did not even know?

The whole set-up was an enigma which presented no clues. The only thing that made sense about the night's mad events was the motive back of the Black Wolf's order that Raine be murdered and his corpse hidden in an unmarked grave back in the Chihuahua badlands.

All star-toters were automatically the enemies of the Black Wolf, potential barriers to that outlaw's smuggling activities. It mattered not that Raine's presence in the Mexitex area had no bearing whatsoever on the Black Wolf's Border-hopping. It was enough that his henchmen, by reason of mistaken identity, had delivered an American tin-star to his lair.

The third Mexican was waiting in the shadow-clotted alley with the horses. For a moment the trio conversed rapidly in Spanish, addressing the man with the horses as "Pancho," and explaining the Black Wolf's reaction to their captive.

Back in saddle, Clay Raine saw that the Black Wolf's gunhawks made no effort to blindfold him. This was an ominous sign. It bore out the fact that this was to be a one-way ride for their prisoner.

His pupils widened in the inky night, Raine attempted to spot landmarks which would tell him where he was. They were riding away from an adobe-walled saloon, with grass growing from fissures in its red-tiled roof. Facing the saloon on the opposite side of the alley was the sheer wall of a two-story *posada* building.

Pancho galloped away into the darkness when they had reached the outskirts of the town, threading through narrow, foul-smelling lanes bordered by wattle huts and canvas-roofed hovels of the poorer population.

Floriado and Esteban, riding at Raine's stirrups, and with Esteban dallying a hackamore about his saddle-horn to prevent Raine from attempting a getaway on the trail ahead, set out toward the serrated backdrop of the Chihuahua malpais.

They climbed steadily up a series of switch-backs until they had topped a ridge overlooking the Mexican town. Hipping about in saddle, Clay Raine believed he had his bearings, for he could see the twinkling lights of a settlement on the Texas side, reflected in the sluggish, muddy current of the Rio Grande. He thought he knew where he was now.

In all probability, he had not been unconscious for long. The Mexican trio had spirited him out of Mexitex on a horse provided for them, no doubt, by their accomplice who held down a hostler's job with the Trail House.

They had crossed the Rio Grande at a point safe from the surveillance of the Border patrol riders, then had doubled back to Coyotero. But it gave Clay Raine scant solace to know that he was probably the only lawman alive who knew that the Black Wolf made his headquarters in a Coyotero saloon. That information would be of no value to him in another hour, when Esteban and Floriado were pouring the clods over his lifeless body.

The lights of the sprawling twin towns on either bank of the Rio Grande dropped out of sight behind the cactus-studded ridge as they headed off toward the south.

A lopsided moon, pale and ghastly as an eye in a corpse, lifted over the Sierra Caliente crags fifteen minutes later, bathing the Mexican wilderness in a greenish witch-glow. At a point where the trail dipped down into a shadowy canyon, the Mexicans halted up and proceeded to roll cigarettes whose odor acquainted Raine with the fact that his captors were *marijuana* addicts.

After a ten-minute wait the Mexicans were rejoined by Pancho. The Texan grimaced involuntarily as he saw what Pancho had been dispatched to obtain—a short-handled shovel, of a type used by prospectors. Only in this case, the tool would be used to dig a grave.

"The Black Wolf takes no chances, *compañeros*!" Pancho addressed his partners in Mexican, when they had resumed their trek down into the twisting canyon. "He is coming out to Tequila Cañon later tonight, to make sure we bury this gringo deep and well. It would not do for the *rurales* to know we killed a Texicano lawman tonight, no."

Below the frowning rim-rocks of Tequila Canyon, the riders were forced to string out single file and fight their way through crowding chaparral. It tore at Clay Raine's exposed face and threatened to rip off his gag.

There were plenty of side canyons, up which the American saw chances of making his escape. But the hackamore of his pony's head-stall was still dallied to Esteban's saddle-horn, and the deputy noted that all three of the Mexicans kept a gun out of holster, against any attempt at a break.

Phantom moonlight shafted down into the arid arroyo as they reached a sandy clearing hemmed in by beetling *tufa* cliffs. The blind box end of Tequila Canyon was Clay Raine's appointed spot of doom, and the lawman felt his muscles stiffen with apprehension as the peon trio reined up and swung from stirrups.

Plainly under the influence of the drug they had consumed through their doped cigarettes, the Mexicans exchanged jokes and cavorted like striplings as they hauled Raine from saddle and advanced out onto the moon-drenched clearing.

Pancho brought up the grave-digging shovel and set

to work at a spot indicated by Esteban, leader of the group.

As Pancho began gouging out a grave in the hard-packed earth, Esteban hefted his long-barreled six-gun and strode around in front of their Texican prisoner, a broad grin exposing his battery of yellow-stained, fanglike teeth.

"Eet ees *muy malo* for you that you ride the palomino eento Mexitex tonight, senor," Esteban chuckled, with a mock bow. "The Black Wolf, he expect someone else, *si.* But the star on your *camisa*—la! Eet make no deeference. The gringo who veesits the Black Wolf een his den, he die anyhow. Eet ees only better that our mistake was made on the gringo law, savvy?"

Pancho paused in his shoveling as he saw Esteban step back, lifting his six-gun and drawing a bead on Clay Raine's chest.

Raine glanced desperately about him. With his arms tied behind him, it would be impossible to resist. But his legs were unshackled, and there were handy side draws to make for. Even though it was suicidal, Raine preferred to be bullet-butchered attempting escape, rather than stand as meek as a *ladrone* before a firing squad and eat lead.

Swinging into a crouch, Clay Raine was in the act of leaping into a sprint when Pancho called out sharply:

"Wait, Esteban *amigo*! For why do we kill the gringo dog now? This grave, she is hard work to dig. The earth is full of rocks, and Pancho's back is already sore."

Esteban lowered his gun, rubbing his stubbled jaw thoughtfully as he pondered Pancho's hint.

Clay Raine relaxed, as a sudden plan burst upon him. To make a break for it now would mean certain death before the blazing guns of this dope-addicted threesome.

In the moonlight, at point-blank range, they could not possibly miss. But if his life was to be spared, even temporarily, there was a chance.

"You are right, *hermano*!" boomed Esteban, his paunch shaking with unholy mirth. "*Porque* should we get blisters on our hands, digging a grave for this Texican mongrel?"

Pouching his six-gun, Esteban reached under his shirt collar and drew a long-bladed *cuchillo* from a hidden scabbard. Walking around behind his prisoner, the pot-bellied Mexican sawed the blade over the rawhide thongs which pinioned Raine's arms behind his back. The Texan felt his hands pulse with new life as the constriction ceased and blood flowed once more into his fingers. Pancho, grinning like a bull gorilla, strode forward and held out the shovel.

"Texan, dig your grave!" snarled the Mexican. "Dig it deep and wide, my gringo frien'. And *andale*—the job must be feeneesh' before the Black Wolf comes!"

Rubbing his chafed wrists, Clay Raine reached up and tore out the gag which had drawn blood from the corners of his mouth. He sucked in a grateful breath as he reached out to accept the shovel from Pancho.

"Listen, you devils!" Raine panted hoarsely, glancing about at the three Mexicans, ignoring the gun bores which were leveled at his brisket. "I'll make you a deal. Spare my life, and you will get *oro*—lots of it. I've got—"

Floriado laughed contemptuously.

"You got *dinero* een a money-belt, no?" jeered the smuggler. "You mean you *deed* have *dinero,* senor. We took your gold before we took you out of Pablo's livery barn een Mexitex. Your bribe, it no work with the Black Wolf's *compadres*."

Raine's shoulders slumped in well-feigned resignation. He stumbled out into the clearing, gripped the shovel handle doggedly, and set to work.

Digging his own grave! Raine's bleeding lips twisted in a cryptic smile as he attacked the hard earth, kicking the shovel blade into the adobe with a spike-heeled boot.

The three Mexicans squatted down a few feet away, like buzzards awaiting a feast. Other *marijuana* cigarettes were lighted, and the peons whiled away the passing minutes taunting their prisoner.

An hour's work brought the outlines of the grave into view—three feet wide, six feet long, A foot beneath the surface of the canyon floor, the going was easier with the hardpan clods removed, and the shovel blade gouging into the moist sand.

One thing the Mexicans could not fathom. Their prisoner seemed to be trying to rush the digging of his own grave, though the *tonto* fool must know that when it reached its prescribed depth, a bullet in the head would mark finis to his endeavors.

Yet the muscular Texan worked as if the devil himself were overseeing the job. He stripped off his vest and shirt, revealing a muscle-slabbed back. Sweat gleamed in the moon rays, as Clay Raine sunk the grave knee-deep and kept going, not pausing for rest as his shovel dug rhythmically into the yielding earth, adding to the mound of dirt alongside the hole.

The narcotic-deadened Mexicans did not notice that their victim was piling the mound of earth between them and the grave.

CHAPTER 4

Three Dying Words

TWO HOURS AFTER THE MEXICANS HAD TURNED OVER the back-breaking task to their prisoner, Clay Raine was standing hip-deep in the oblong grave. He paused, lungs heaving, to run splayed fingers through his shock of sweat-sopped, reddish hair.

Esteban lumbered to his feet from the reclining position he had enjoyed for the past forty minutes. His companions eyed the beefy Mexican indifferently as he waddled over to one end of the grave to inspect its depth.

"You are but half through, Senor Tejano," declared Esteban, twirling his Colt .45 by the trigger guard. "Bury you deep—those were the orders of the Black Wolf—"

In that instant the panting Texan flew into action like a bursting bomb. Stooping quickly, he swept up a dirt-laden shovel, to send the full brunt of the moist sand blasting into Esteban's face.

With a snort of terror, Esteban clapped his free hand to his face, clawing sand from his eyes. Instantly Raine's shovel blade stabbed like a bayonet into the Mexican's paunch, doubling him up with agony.

Wham! A clubbing uppercut jarred Esteban's jaw, and the blow rendered the Mexican helpless as he felt the Texan's hands clawing at the six-gun in his lax fingers.

Floriado and Pancho bounced to their feet with hoarse yells of alarm, as they saw moon rays wink on the pistol barrel which Raine slammed with crushing force over

Esteban's skull.

Brain tissue oozed from the Mexican's head as he flopped back. And in that instant, the *marijuana*-incensed outlaws saw the cunning back of their victim's grave digging.

Even as Floriado and Pancho whipped six-guns from holsters, Clay Raine ducked out of sight in the half-dug grave. Their slugs ripped harmlessly into the barrier of dirt Raine had piled up between them!

Tequila Canyon resounded to an ear-shattering thunder of shots, as Clay Raine crouched low in the half-dug grave. His eyes shuttled along the crest of the mound of dirt which was absorbing the Mexican duo's bullets as effectively as the backstop of a pistol target.

A bleak grin twisted the Texan's mouth as he heard the shooting break off, followed by an exchange of panic-stricken whispering between Floriado and Pancho. Obviously, they were holding a council of war.

Risking a bullet, Raine straightened, thrusting his gun across the heap of excavated dirt. He thumbed a slug in the direction of the two peons, who had withdrawn to the base of the *tufa* cliff where their horses had been hobbled.

Pancho howled a Mexican oath as Raine's slug clipped the muscle of his forearm, spinning him half around. Floriado answered with a thunderous burst of shots from his Colt, bullets which kicked sand in Raine's face and forced him to duck back into his excavation.

The Texas lawman cursed his luck. Given his own Peacemaker, his snap-shot, fast as he had sent it, would have tallied Floriado dead center, instead of nipping his arm. But Esteban's .45 had the wrong "feel," and its trigger pull was unfamiliar.

Aware that their prisoner had reversed the odds against them by his lightning-swift attack on Esteban, and that Raine might easily stand off a siege from his own grave until the moon had westered behind the Tequila Canyon rim, Floriado and Pancho separated.

Pancho headed down the canyon, crouched low, his face taut from the pain of the bleeding bullet-furrow on his arm. His *compadre,* hugging the cliff, circled the box end of the gorge in an effort to gain an elevated position, from which vantage point he could expose Raine to a murderous fire from the rear.

Squatting tensely in the half-dug grave, his pulse hammering like a rabbit's, the Texan strained his ears to follow the movements of his two adversaries. Obviously, Floriado and Pancho intended to catch him between cross-fires, trusting to one or the other of them being able to bag their target.

Raine had the advantage of a trench to hide in. But he knew the odds were against his leaving the grave alive.

A quick inspection of the cylinder of Esteban's gun showed an empty chamber, kept under the firing pin when the gun reposed in holster. One empty shell, with which he had pinked one of his foemen a moment before. That left four cartridges.

"Two's all I need," he thought tightly, "but they ain't apt to get out in the moonlight where I can draw a sure bead."

A rattling in the alluvial rubble at the box end of the canyon told Raine that Floriado was scrambling up the crumpled talus, undoubtedly keeping behind the cover of boulders, to gain a view of the open grave. Of Pancho, Raine had heard nothing for several minutes. But it was too much to hope for that Pancho had been put out of commission by Raine's first shot.

Esteban had a second gun, but Raine saw that the man he had clubbed to death had fallen on the holster, and he could not risk exposing himself to roll the Mexican's two-hundred-pound bulk to clear the holstered .45.

Raine's nerves were on edge, his whole body trembling from the severe manual labor he had undergone in digging the grave at top speed. But the grueling effort had been well-planned. Still Raine knew that if he were to get any break at all, it must come before the Black Wolf arrived on his scheduled visit to inspect the grave.

The moon was not due to set beyond the Tequila Canyon rim for another twenty minutes. With the coming of darkness, Raine knew he had a good chance of leaving the grave and seeking out his Mexican besiegers, carrying the fight to them.

But Floriado and Pancho were reckoning on that strategy likewise. The Mexicans were staking all on being able to kill Raine where he crouched, before the Black Wolf's arrival. They were already quaking at the prospects of Black Wolf's wrath, when the smuggler learned of Esteban's death.

Wriggling his way up the talus rocks which had fallen from the brink of the box canyon, Floriado squirmed about and scanned the floor of the gorge immediately below him. Moon rays gilded the edges of the rectangular grave where Clay Raine was crouching deep in shadow. Somewhere further down the canyon, Pancho was probably working his way into an elevated position where he could open fire on the game Texan—

Floriado inched his way upward, resting his six-gun muzzle across a *tufa* fragment. His body was protected by the shadow cast by the beetling cliff rim overhead, but his Colt was exposed to the moon's rays.

Unknowingly, Floriado had crucified his chances of ending the fight. Clay Raine, his eyes sweeping the surrounding cliffs in all directions, caught the sight of a wink of moonlight on gun-steel, marking the spot where Floriado had climbed.

Raine's borrowed gun slanted upward across the rim of the grave. For a brief instant his eyes squinted up the gunsights, taking a medium notch on the invisible Mexican behind the exposed gun up amid the talus.

Spang! The Colt recoiled savagely in Raine's grasp. Through a fount of gunsmoke, the bayed lawman saw Floriado's dark bulk rear up behind the talus rock. Cutting through the smashing echoes of the shot, the Texan heard Floriado's muffled groan of agony.

Then Floriado staggered out into the open, fumbling with his left hand at a bullet-shattered collar bone. The Mexican was struggling to bring his gun to a level.

Bracing himself inside the grave's walls, Clay Raine let gun-hammer drop on firing pin. He saw Floriado sprawl back against the talus before the impact of a second slug—this time a dead-center shot to the Mexican's breast-bone.

Toppling forward, Floriado rolled down the talus pile to sprawl motionless on the floor of the canyon, just out of Raine's vision.

A ghastly silence filled Tequila Canyon for a moment, then was broken by a sound of slogging boots down the gorge, as Pancho headed back toward the clearing.

"*Amigo*!" came Pancho's tentative call. "The *Tejano* is dead?"

Clay Raine whirled about in the half-dug grave and

eared back his gun prong in readiness to meet his surviving foe. A grim smile flickered across his bloody lips as he called back, imitating Floriado's oily voice as best he could:

"*Seguromente,* Pancho!"

There was a moment's silence, and Raine wondered if his ruse would bring Pancho into the open. Then he caught sight of the remaining Mexican, stalking cautiously out into the moonlight, twin Colts leveled at the yawning grave.

Raine swung to a crouching position in the grave, moon rays glinting off his smoke-spewing Colt. The shadow of the gun-muzzle fell across Esteban's corpse as Raine stood in full view of the approaching Pancho.

Too late, Pancho realized that he had been tricked. His bulging eyes caught a glimpse of Floriado's corpse, sprawled at the base of the talus. Then he went into action, triggering both Colts in unison.

One slug ripped into Esteban's back. Another gouged a long furrow along the wall of the grave where Raine stood.

Staking all on a single shot, Raine stood his ground for a fleeting interval, unwilling to gamble on a wild shot, as had Pancho. Flame spat from Raine's gun bore. Before the canyon wind had whipped away the spout of white smoke, the American deputy saw that his aim had been unerringly true.

With a gagged oath, Pancho buckled at the knees and pitched sideward to the ground. Mortally wounded, Pancho was struggling to prop himself up on one elbow, trigger his guns once more. But Clay Raine was already in action, vaulting out of the grave and sprinting for the shadow of the canyon wall beyond Esteban's corpse.

With one bullet left in his gun, Raine approached Pancho's sprawled body with pantherlike wariness. He came upon Pancho from the side and kicked the Mexican's guns to one side.

Rolling over on his back, Pancho clawed at the bullet-hole in his chest, near the heart. Crimson bubbles grew and burst on Pancho's lips as he gasped hoarsely:

"*Agua*—water, senor! I burn up eenside—*agua*—"

Raine felt compassion for the dope-fiend groveling at his feet. Hurrying over to Pancho's horse, he unslung a canteen from the pommel and returned to the Mexican's side, unscrewing the cap and letting the dying outlaw swig deep.

"*Gracias—amigo*," wheezed Pancho, his head sagging to the ground.

Raine put a hand on the outlaw's shoulder. "Tell me, *pelado*," he asked. "How come the Black Wolf wanted me captured? Who's this here Gideon Rassmussen you hombres mistook me for?"

Pancho lifted his head, and seemed spent with the effort. Three words gusted from his throat, sounding like gibberish to Raine:

"The—Golden—Spur!"

A shudder racked Pancho, and he was dead.

CHAPTER 5

Trail to Mexitex

INTENDING TO WALK OVER TO FLORIADO AND MAKE sure he had killed the Mexican, the American lawman was on his feet when, with bewildering unexpectedness, a thunder of swift hoofs swept up the canyon. A lone rider rounded the bend, coming in full view of the death-scene ahead.

The Black Wolf!

Raine got off a shot from the hip, emptying Esteban's Colt. The slug missed, but it caused the Black Wolf to halt his mustang.

In desperation, Clay Raine flung aside the empty revolver and leaped to snatch up one of Pancho's .45s. He saw the white-masked smuggler chief hauling a carbine from his saddle-boot, as the Black Wolf spotted the three bodies of his slain henchmen, and realized that by some miracle their prisoner had shot his way to freedom.

A cold laugh jarred Raine as he braced himself for shoot-out. He saw the Black Wolf lever a shell into the Winchester breech. An instant later Tequila Canyon rocked to the roar of the .30-30.

The screaming steel-jacketed missile plucked the bullhide batwing of Raine's left chap-leg, but the next second found him diving into the shelter of jet-black shadow under the cliff wall.

The range was far for six-gun work, but Clay Raine opened fire at the silhouetted horse and rider down the canyon.

With slugs screaming about him and ricocheting off the *tufa* walls, the Black Wolf sized up the situation as suicidal to himself. His only way of reaching the blind end of Tequila Canyon was through the moonlit corridor between the cliffs, and Clay Raine, protected by darkness, could bag his target without undue risk to himself.

An oath of disappointment ground through Raine's beard as he saw the Black Wolf wheel his mustang about and roll the hooks. The Rio Grande smuggler had chosen flight to showdown.

Whirling, Clay Raine sprinted back to where the three Mexicans had hobbled their horses. Quickly jerking the rawhide noose from the forelegs of the buckskin which had been his mount to and from Coyotero, Raine jerked the latigo tight and swung into saddle.

A moment later he was hammering out of Tequila Canyon, Pancho's six-guns in his holsters. Ahead of him on the brushy trail, the dust of the Black Wolf's getaway eddied in the moonlight.

"That smugglin' hombre is prob'ly lightin' a shuck to Coyotero. If I can overhaul him on this buckskin mebbe I can square accounts yet!"

Pounding out of the chaparral-choked mouth of Tequila Canyon, Raine glimpsed his adversary topping the next rise. By spurring the buckskin at a reckless clip out of the gorge, Raine had cut down the Black Wolf's lead a trifle. But it became apparent, by the heavy breathing of the horse under him as they hammered up the ridge slope, that the Black Wolf was better mounted tonight.

The dust of a top-gallop flight was visible along the cactus-dotted backbone of the hilltop as Raine gained the summit. Already, his buckskin was faltering. From what he had seen of the Black Wolf's mustang, Raine knew that the Rio Grande Border-hopper had every chance of making his getaway.

"He may hole up and try ambushin' me," Raine told himself, as he lashed the buckskin into an unwilling gallop. following the Black Wolf's dust-clouded trail. "It ain't likely the Wolf will cotton to sparin' my life, seein' what I done to his three Mex friends."

But from time to time in the hour which followed, the

Texas lawman caught frequent glimpses of the smuggler. The Black Wolf was showing no signs of wanting to invite a showdown with his pursuer. He was heading due north, keeping in the open as much as possible, and avoiding dangerous ledge trails or shadow-clotted barrancas.

"Looks like he's headin' direct for the Rio Grande, instead of Coyotero," mused Raine, as he caught sight of the black gulf of the river's canyon to the northward. "That would seem like the Black Wolf's tryin' to reach Texas instead of Coyotero."

The moon was westering toward the skyline before Raine caught sight of the Rio Grande. The Black Wolf's trail led straight to the muddy flats rimming the Chihuahua side of the river, but the angle of the moonbeams gave Raine a clear view of the Texas bank. The sprawling mesa slope across the Rio harbored no rock nests or chaparral where the Black Wolf could have holed-up for a drygulch shot at his pursuer, and yet there was no sign of the mounted smuggler.

Raine gigged the lather-flanked buckskin down to the water's edge. In the moonlight, he had no difficulty in seeing where the Black Wolf had spurred his mustang straight into the muddy stream, heading for the Texas bank.

This was contrary to all of Raine's figuring. Sooner or later, he believed that the smuggling king would head eastward toward Coyotero, and the saloon where he holed-up. But the trail did not confirm this reasoning.

Aware that he was risking an ambush from the Wolf's long-range .30-30, Raine spurred the Mexican buckskin out into the shallow current. A few minutes later he landed on the Texas side, and picked up the Black Wolf's muddy trail leading downstream along the sand spits.

"Seems to be makin' for Mexitex," mused the cowboy lawman, giving up his efforts to spur the jaded buckskin into a gait faster than a trot. "The Black Wolf owes his life to a fast pony tonight."

The pale promise of a new dawn was pinking the eastern skyline by the time Clay Raine topped a hogback and sighted the tarpaper roofs of Mexitex ahead of him. The Black Wolf had ridden down to the stagecoach road which Raine had traveled the day before, and Raine knew that tracking the outlaw would be impossible in the maze of hoofprints on the road.

Dismounting on the outskirts of town, Raine led the weary buckskin into a draw facing the Rio Grande. Cottonwoods and dwarf willow choked the draw, and provided an ideal hide-out for his horse.

Stripping off the saddle, Raine tied the exhausted pony to a cottonwood. Then, pausing to check the loads in Pancho's guns and replacing spent shells with cartridges from his own belt loops, the deputy marshal headed into Mexitex on foot.

No one was stirring in the cowtown as he headed through the scattered shacks on the outskirts. Saloons and dance-halls had locked up for the night.

The dark hour just preceding sunrise had been given over to night owls and the croaking of bullfrogs on the Rio Grande bottomland.

Thoughts churned in Raine's head as he worked his way toward the rambling, two-story frame building which he remembered as being the Trail House.

Events had moved swiftly since his arrival in Mexitex, only eight hours before. But many an unsolved riddle had entered Clay Raine's life in that brief space of time.

He still did not know the identity of the cowgirl who had greeted him with a mistaken kiss the moment of his arrival in the Rio Grande cow-town. But he did know that she had been expecting the arrival of an uncle on a palomino horse—an uncle she had not seen for a long time, if at all. Otherwise, she would not have mistaken him for Rassmussen.

Whoever Rassmussen was, he had been ticketed for Boot Hill by the outlaw forces ramrodded by the Black Wolf. Somewhere in the tangled skein of events, a "Golden Spur" was a factor. Pancho's enigmatical words, gasped out a few seconds before he died over in Tequila Canyon, pointed to that.

Pancho had mentioned Golden Spur. And the Black Wolf had removed Raine's spurs and nicked at their rowels with a jack-knife, over in the Coyotero saloon.

Reminiscing, Clay Raine recalled the Black Wolf's disappointment, upon scraping the metal from his rowels, to find that they were ordinary iron. Could it mean that the Rio Grande smuggler believed the spur should have been made of gold?

"Huh—a golden spur wouldn't be worth much, anyway," Raine muttered, as he crossed vacant lots to approach the Trail House from the rear. "The Black Wolf wouldn't leave some of his gunslingers waiting for a man, just to get his spurs. There's somethin' more important back of all this mess than just a golden spur."

Waning moonlight gave Raine a view of the horse corrals behind the Trail House stables. The lawman worked his way along the corral fence until he came to the rear of the barn where he had been attacked.

Ducking between the peeled-pole rails, Clay Raine entered the barn through a back door. Odors of horse-flesh and stable smells greeted his nostrils, as he worked his way along a row of stalls.

A familiar whicker greeted him, and a moment later Raine was stroking Palomar's glossy neck.

"Reckon I'll leave yuh bedded down here for the time bein', old hoss," Raine whispered in the palomino's ear. "Wouldn't be surprised if that hostler who stuck a knife in my ribs last night isn't sleepin' somewheres about, and he wouldn't cotton to me movin' yuh out of this barn without payin' yore keep."

Through the Stygian darkness of the stable, Clay Raine picked his way past the spot where the Black Wolf's trio of Mexicans had waylaid him. After a lengthy pause, during which he strained his ears to pick up possible snoring from the stable tender whom he knew must be making his sleeping quarters inside the barn, Raine took a match from his chaps pocket and lighted it.

Luck was with him. His saddle was hanging from a hickory peg behind Palomar's manger, and his *alforja* bags were on the stable floor beneath the kack.

Extinguishing the match, Clay Raine groped through the darkness and obtained his saddlebags. Heaving them over a naked shoulder, he made his way back to the rear door of the barn, and a few moments later was straddling through the corral fence bars.

CHAPTER 6

Circle Spear Cowgirl

SUNRISE WAS GILDING THE CHIHUAHUA MOUNTAINS across the Rio Grande by the time Raine had worked his way back to the draw where he had left the Mexican pony. The sun burst in ruddy splendor over the Texas skyline as Raine tossed his saddle-bags on the ground inside the draw, and unbuckled them.

As he had surmised, the Mexicans who had attacked him the night before had ransacked the saddle-bags in search of plunder. They had found nothing of particular value, for they had already stripped him of the gold-laden money-belt he wore next to his skin.

As daylight strengthened, Raine took out his shaving tools and extra clothing—a scarlet rodeo shirt, spare levis, cowboots which he ordinarily wore only to dances or on Sunday visits to town.

He obtained water from the river nearby and worked up a cold lather with his shaving brush, rubbing the suds into his inch-long growth of beard. It would be a painful job, shaving his wiry growth of whiskers without hot water, but Raine dared not risk building a campfire.

Half an hour later the beard was off, revealing a darkly handsome face and a thin, rust-red mustache following the line of his upper lip. The general effect, viewed in his cracked shaving mirror, was not bad. At any rate, he bore little resemblance to the bearded stranger who had ridden into Mexitex the night before—and straight into a Border mystery.

He stripped off his chocolate-colored batwings with their distinctive R initials worked in brass studs, and donned fresh bibless overalls and his Sunday boots. His vest and shirt had been left beside the half-dug grave over in Tequila Canyon, on the Mexican side of the Rio, so Raine replaced them with the gaudy rodeo shirt with its crescent-shaped pockets.

"Reckon I'm disguised sufficient." The deputy marshal chuckled as he strapped on his gun harness and settled Pancho's Colts in his basketwoven holsters. "I should be able to run smack into the Black Wolf with my beard off and dressed in these duds, and never be recognized."

Heading out of the draw and walking briskly toward the outskirts of Mexitex, Clay Raine was not exactly sure, in his own mind, just why he had elected to stick around Mexitex.

The day before, he had been an ordinary lawman, headed for Laredo to resign the law job he had filled for the past five years. In New Mexico, just over the line from El Paso, he had purchased a small-tally cattle spread three weeks before, and meant to devote his time in the future to that.

Cattle ranching had always been his first love. His boyhood had been spent on his sire's Rocking R spread over in the Panhandle country. He had carefully saved his wages as a federal deputy, against the day when he could make a down payment on a ranch of his own, and finding the Circle X outfit in New Mexico had spelled the discovery of his heart's desire.

The Circle X was now registered in his name. And a herd of feeders was already moving out of Arizona, consigned to his ranch.

The last chapter in his law career lay ahead of him, in his trek to Laredo to turn over his badge. But that mission had carried him into Mexitex the day before.

"I must be loco," he grunted, as he headed down the spur-scuffed wooden sidewalk of the main street, making in the direction of the Trail House and Mexitex's only restaurant. "I could easy as not have choused Palomar out of that stable, and be on my way to Laredo by now. Instead I'm tryin' to stick my horns into this here Rassmussen's trouble with the Black Wolf. Be blamed if I know why."

But Raine knew he was kidding himself. A pair of larkspur blue eyes and the memory of a kiss which had not been meant for him at all was the motive he had for sticking around Mexitex today.

That, plus an unsettled score with the Black Wolf—and the unraveling of the riddle of the Golden Spur, which seemed to be back of the murder trap he had escaped in Chihuahua.

Passing the livery barn where he had been attacked the night before, Clay Raine stiffened as he caught sight of the hostler who had thrust a knife in his ribs, obviously working in collusion with the Black Wolf's henchmen. The Mexican youth was assisting a cowboy to mount a pony which had been stabled in the barn overnight. The waddy was obviously the worse off for a hard bout with red-eye the night before.

As Raine strode past, the hostler's eyes met his. But the stable boy gave no sign of recognition. Catching sight of his own reflection in a hotel window as he mounted the porch steps of the Trail House, Raine took comfort from the fact that he bore little resemblance to the bearded, trail-dusty man who had arrived in Mexitex the preceding dusk.

Not having eaten since noon the day before, Clay Raine entered the cow-town hotel and crossed the lobby to a restaurant adjoining. In short order he was getting outside a breakfast of java, steaming fried spuds, and a man-sized plate of eggs and sowbelly.

He was enjoying his third cup of coffee when the hotel lobby door opened and Raine caught sight of the girl who had greeted him the evening before. Apparently she had spent the night in town, at the Trail House.

Raine feasted his eyes on her, noting details which had escaped him on the occasion of their brief meeting. She was dressed the same—apricot-colored blouse with horseshoe designs embroidered on the pockets, and a silken scarf looped about her throat. She wore a cream-colored Stetson and a split-type doeskin riding skirt. Her feet looked trim in polished taffy-brown boots equipped with nickeled spurs.

Raine noted, with brows arching in surprise, that she had double-shell belts buckled about her waist, and pearl-handled six-shooters in holsters swung low on her trim thighs. The lawman knew from the cut of those scabbards that the Colts—low-calibered though they were, being .32s—were not worn merely for ornament.

"Mornin', Miss Grace!" sang out the bald-headed cook, busy rattling dishes behind an aperture in the kitchen wall behind the counter where Raine was seated on a stool. "did that uncle of yores show up?"

The girl shook her head, removing her Stetson and shaking back a wealth of chestnut tresses. She seated herself in a wall booth at the far end of the restaurant.

"No—worse luck!" she answered, in a melodious voice which stirred Raine to the core. "I'm worried about him, Dud. He was due day before yesterday or yesterday morning at the latest. I can't imagine what's keeping him."

Raine tarried over his coffee during the time it took the cook to serve the girl breakfast. When the white-aproned restaurant man brought him his change, Raine leaned over the counter and asked in a voice too low to reach the girl's ears:

"Is that Rassmussen's niece yonder, *amigo*?"

The restaurant owner nodded.

"Shore is, cowboy. Grace Spear, her name is. You a friend of Gid Rassmussen's?"

Raine shook his head.

"No. But I—"

The waiter bustled away to take care of an influx of new customers. Unstraddling from the counter stool, Raine was intending to walk over to Grace Spear's booth when he saw that the girl had breakfasted on a single cup of coffee and was now heading for the street door.

Pausing on the threshold, she called to the restaurant man:

"I'm going over to the barn to get my pony, Dud. If my uncle should show up in the next few minutes, tell him I'll be over at Kim Hitchcock's bank, will you? I've got an appointment with Kim before I ride back to the ranch."

Dud grinned paternally from behind the counter.

"I shore will, Grace. Yuh reckon yore uncle will ask here for yuh, though?"

Grace Spear nodded, and Clay Raine could see the troubled lights in her eyes.

"Yes. I told him I'd meet him at the Trail House, instead of at the ranch."

The screen door fanned shut on the girl's departing figure, and Raine hurried after her. Out on the hotel porch, he hesitated as he saw her making for the livery barn next door.

"Might be risky to talk to her in front of that Mex hostler," he decided. "He might recognize my voice. Reckon I can hang around the bank until she comes out. She's got to be warned that the Black Wolf's gang is layin' for Rassmussen."

Remembering that he had left his sombrero inside the restaurant, Raine went back inside. He found Dud eyeing the change for a five-dollar bill which Raine, in his haste, had left on the counter.

"Right big tip yuh left me for a six-bit breakfast, son." Dud grinned, scooping in the coins. "Cowhands hardly ever tip, anyhow. Drummers usually do, and city dudes. *Muchas gracias,* stranger."

The deputy grinned ruefully as he saw the waiter pocket the money. It represented the only pocket *dinero* he had to his name, since the Black Wolf's Mexicans had stolen his money-belt. Except for a government pay-check in his pocket, which he would have to cash, he was dead broke.

"Yuh mentioned Gid Rassmussen, stranger," continued the friendly waiter. "Miss Spear has been waitin' for him to show up for two days now. Terrible important, judgin' from the way she's actin'. Yuh know why Rassmussen ain't arrived?"

Raine met the restaurant man's level stare, and mentally ticketed Dud for a man he could trust.

Obviously he was an old friend of Grace Spear's.

"No—matter of fact, I've never met Rassmussen," he countered. "Reason I asked yuh if she was Gid's niece was—a—because I overheard yuh ask her if he'd showed up yet."

Dud frowned, as if puzzling out the riddle of this stranger's relationship to Rassmussen.

"Could yuh tell me where she lives, feller?" asked Raine, trying to make his voice sound casual as he fished in his rodeo shirt for tobacco and thin husks. "I—I got some news about her uncle that I'd like to tell her in person."

Dud scooped together Raine's breakfast dishes.

"Grace owns the Circle Spear Ranch north of town," he replied. "Her old man, Cunnel Christopher Spear, was murdered a year ago by the Black Wolf when Spear caught the Wolf rustlin' some of his Circle Spear stock across the Rio. Since then she's been tryin' to carry on for the cunnel."

Seeing that Dud was momentarily unoccupied, and in a talkative mood, Raine pressed his questioning further.

"Kind of tough job for a young girl, ain't it? Ramroddin' a cattle ranch?"

Dud waggled his head somberly.

"You hit the nail on the head, hombre. The Black Wolf's mighty nigh stripped her spread of beef steers, since her dad was bushwhacked. The Stockman's Bank holds a heavy mortgage on the Circle Spear, and it falls due any day now, I understand."

Raine pursed his lips thoughtfully, remembering that Grace Spear had an appointment at the Mexitex bank this morning.

"As a matter of fact, that's why she sent for Gid Rassmussen," the restaurant man went on. "He's her mother's brother—an old prospector. Never been in Mexitex that I know of. But it seems like Rassmussen struck it rich lately, and Grace figgered as how he might buy up the bank's paper and give her a chance to restock the Circle Spear."

Hoofbeats clattered on the street outside, and Raine turned to see Grace Spear leaving the stable astride a strawberry roan cowpony. She was heading up the street.

"There she goes now, son," Dud said. "Yuh can catch her over at the bank, before she leaves town."

Raine thanked the waiter and picked up his hat,

figuring that the four-dollar “tip” which Dud had appropriated had been money well spent.

CHAPTER 7

Kidnap Attempt

WHAT LITTLE THE RESTAURANT MAN HAD TOLD HIM regarding Grace Spear bore out Clay Raine’s hunch that the cowgirl was in desperate trouble of some kind. A prospector uncle, Gid Rassmussen, was due to arrive in Mexitex to lend her financial assistance.

“But when Rassmussen does show up, the Black Wolf’s gang will be waitin’ for him—unless they’ve already ’gulched him, which same could be the reason why Rassmussen’s overdue.”

Leaving the wooden-awninged porch, Raine walked up the street, his eyes fixed on Grace Spear. The girl had reined her strawberry roan before a hitch-rack in front of a false-fronted frame shack bearing a weatherbeaten sign that read:

STOCKMAN’S BANK
Kimball Hitchcock, Pres.

Few persons were stirring in Mexitex at this early hour, and Raine saw the Circle Spear cowgirl hitch her pony and walk up on the bank porch, settling herself on a bench beside the door. She seemed preoccupied and distraught.

“Reckon now’s my chance to have a pow-wow with Grace.” Raine grinned, hastening his steps. “She got a good look at me in the Trail House restaurant, and didn't appear to know she'd ever seen me before. Which is downright impolite, seein' as how she give me a kiss."

As he approached the cowtown bank, Raine was reminded that he had a U.S. pay-check to cash. His Mexican attackers had spared him his law badge, but it was on the shirt over in Tequila Canyon at the moment, and therefore, useless as a means of identification.

However, he had never encountered any trouble cashing his government drafts, and the check he carried in his pocket now would be sorely needed by the time he had to pay for his next meal.

Swinging up the bank steps, Raine doffed his Stetson as he saw Grace Spear eye him impersonally from her bench by the door.

"Mornin', ma'am," the deputy marshal greeted. "Could yuh tell me when this here bank opens up?"

The cowgirl smiled at him, and it was obvious from her expression that she did not recall their previous meeting.

"Kim Hitchcock usually shows up around six-thirty," she answered. "Rather early for banker's hours, maybe, but then he takes a four-hour siesta in the middle of the afternoon."

Raine seated himself at the opposite end of the bench and fished in his pocket for a match with which to light his quirly.

Face to face with the girl, Raine found himself at a loss for approaching the topic of her uncle. If she knew that Gid Rassmussen was marked for Boot Hill by the Black Wolf's gunnies, she might well resent his bringing up the subject, for fear that this handsome stranger might be one of the Wolf's lawless legion.

Gulping hard, Raine looked up from lighting his

smoke.

"This mornin' in the restaurant," he began awkwardly, "I heard the waiter ask yuh if yore unc—"

The girl jumped to her feet, oblivious of his presence. Looking up, Clay Raine saw a tall, powerfully built man wearing an El Stroud sombrero and a loose riding coat walking up the bank steps. His bearing was that of an influential citizen.

"Kim!" cried Grace Spear, advancing to meet the well-groomed man. "I'm so glad you are opening the bank ahead of time this morning. I—I've got to see you."

Kimball Hitchcock exposed gold-capped teeth in a smile of greeting as he removed his Stetson.

"Sure enough, Grace!" The banker laughed, reaching in his pocket for a ring of keys. "You aren't paying off your father's mortgage a day before it falls due, by any chance?"

Raine heard the catch in Grace Spear's voice as she answered:

"No, Kim. That—that's what I wanted to see you about. You know I am expecting my Uncle Gid—to help me out. But he—he is more than a day over-due. I'm afraid something's happened to him."

Kimball Hitchcock unlocked the bank door and stood aside for the girl to enter. As Clay Raine stood up, flicking his cigarette into the gutter, he saw the gray-headed banker pause in the act of closing the door.

"You waiting to get in the bank, stranger?" Hitchcock asked eyeing Raine appraisingly from Stetson to cowboots.

"Yeah," the marshal replied, pulling an envelope from his levi pocket. "I'd like to cash a check drawn on

Uncle Sam's treasury."

Raine followed Hitchcock inside. Grace Spear had crossed the bank lobby and seated herself in a leather chair beside a desk bearing a bronze plaque with Hitchcock's name on it.

"This bank ain't in the habit of cashing checks for strangers son," Hitchcock said, taking the check from Raine. "Hmmm . . . Payment for services rendered as a deputy marshal. That's different. We always aim to oblige the law."

Clay Raine tore his gaze from Grace Spear and turned to meet the banker's scrutiny.

"You have your badge and other credentials, of course?" Hitchock said, walking over to a teller's cage and unlocking the grilled door. "Even John Laws need identification here."

Raine presented himself at the window, debating whether to confess that the notorious smuggler, the Black Wolf, had temporarily dispossessed him of his deputy's star. Then he decided to play it safe and remain incognito, insofar as any Mexitex resident was concerned.

"I don't usually carry my badge around in plain sight," Raine countered. "But here's a souvenir from my Rodeo bronc-ridin' days that'll serve to identify me, I reckon. A little brand I picked up a carnival sideshow when I was younger."

As he spoke, Raine rolled back his left sleeve and slid his arm under the grill of the cashier's window. Tattooed in blue ink over the sinew-corded skin was the name "Clay Raine" in a curlicued script.

"Proof enough that you belong to this check," Hitchcock said, handing the marshal a pen. "Just endorse it."

Hitchcock counted out bills and shoved them across the marble slab to the lawman. His eyes searched the cowboy's face interestedly as Raine thanked him.

"Ain't in Mexitex hunting the Black Wolf, by any chance?" Hitchcock inquired off-handedly.

Raine's eyes narrowed. Was Kimball Hitchcock aware of the fact that the smuggler chief made his headquarters across the river in Coyotero? If so, the Mexitex banker had information which the U.S. Border Patrol would pay a heavy bounty to learn.

"No," Raine answered. "I'm just passin' through yore town on my way to Laredo. Why? Is the Black Wolf hereabouts?"

The banker shrugged.

"*Quien sabe?* That outlaw seems to be everywhere along the Rio Grande. At any rate, he's rustled plenty of cattle from ranchers in this country. I just thought, seeing as how you were a Federal deputy, maybe the Black Wolf had been traced to our section of the Big Bend."

Hitchcock came out of the teller's cage and headed over toward his desk, dismissing Raine from his thoughts.

Heading outside, the deputy saw Hitchcock raising a window alongside his desk. Hitchcock's action put an idea into Raine's head.

"A little eavesdroppin' might be *muy bueno* along about now," he muttered. Hurrying down the bank steps, he rounded the corner toward Hitchcock's open window. "Seems like I've drawed chips in Grace Spear's game, an' it might help to know where she stands with that banker dude."

Raine hunkered down below the window, out of sight

in case Hitchcock happened to glance out the window. He heard Hitchcock haul up his swivel chair, clear his throat, and open the discussion.

"Well, little Lady Gracious," Hitchcock said, "what's troubling you?"

Raine heard the girl's intake of breath, the drumming of her fingernails on Hitchcock's desk.

"Kim, I realize my father's note expires tomorrow noon. If I can't meet it, you can legally take over my Circle Spear outfit."

"That's right. Do I infer you haven't the cash to pay off the colonel's mortgage?"

A note of pleading entered Grace's voice.

"Kim, where could I get money, seeing as how the Black Wolf stripped my range of our fall beef gather last year? How—"

Raine heard Hitchcock's swivel chair squeal as the banker toyed with papers on his desk. A plume of mellow cigar smoke drifted through the open window about the squatting lawman.

"You've talked too freely of your affairs around town, Grace," Hitchcock said evasively. "From a dozen sources I've heard gossip about your prospector uncle coming to town, with money to raise your father's debt. If this uncle is coming, why should you worry your little head?"

"Because," she protested bitterly, "Uncle Gid should be—was due in Mexitex day before yesterday. I—I spent all day yesterday waiting for him at the Trail House. I know nothing this side of Hades could keep Uncle Gid from getting here to help me."

There was a moment's pause. Then the banker asked craftily:

"What do you expect me to do if Rassmussen fails to

arrive, Grace? Grant you another extension on your father's note?"

Clay Raine could barely hear the girl's answer.

"Won't you, Kim? For my sake?"

Raine withdrew hastily to a point further down the bank wall as Hitchcock got to his feet and came to the window, staring out at the Mexitex landscape. A cigar was clamped between his gold-capped teeth, and his eyes were as cold and bleak as tarnished silver.

"Business is business, Grace," Hitchcock finally said. "Your father's note was originally due last Christmas. I granted you a six-months' extension, realizing you couldn't pay off after the Black Wolf murdered Colonel Spear and robbed you of your fall beef gather."

"Then—then you plan to foreclose, Kim? Even though you know Uncle Gid is on his way here with the money?"

Hitchcock shrugged and turned back toward his desk.

"I'm afraid that's how it stacks up, Grace," the banker replied coldly. "I can't run a bank on promises."

"But Kim—" The girl's voice broke on a half-sob. "The Circle Spear—it's all I have. You couldn't—"

Hitchcock laughed harshly.

"There is always the easy way out of your difficulty, darling," the banker said, his voice taking on a tender note. "I've asked you repeatedly to be my wife. With the backing of my bank, we could make the Circle Spear invulnerable against the possibility of future raids by the Black Wolf and his Border-hoppers. You have only to say the word, and—"

Grace Spear cut Hitchcock off with a low, poignant cry.

"You—you're old enough to be my father!" she

stormed. “You ought to know I couldn’t marry you unless I loved you. If you think—I’d become your wife just to save Dad’s ranch—”

Raine’s lips compressed with anger as he heard Hitchcock’s grating laughter, then the clatter of Grace Spear’s boot-heels as she fled across the lobby.

Moving swiftly, Clay Raine reached the front of the bank in time to see Grace run out the door, down the steps, and over to the hitch-rack where she had tied her roan. The girl’s cheeks were streaming with tears and her chest was heaving with tumultuous emotion.

“Miss Spear!” Raine called, as he saw her duck under the tie bar and snatch up her pony’s reins. “Just a second, Miss S—”

But the owner of the Circle Spear appeared not to have heard the deputy. She swung into stirrups and curveted the roan out into the street, spurring into a gallop in the direction of the Trail House.

Raine hurried toward the hotel, believing that the girl intended to resume her wait for Gid Rassmussen. Instead, she galloped on toward the street intersection and reined northward.

A moment later Raine saw her lining out down a road which twisted off and away into the Big Bend hills.

“Looks like she’s slopin’ for the home spread,” Raine decided. “I reckon I’ll take a *pasear* out that direction myself. The way I size things up, Grace needs an *amigo*, and needs one bad.”

Raine broke into a run, heading for the secluded draw off the Rio Grande where he had left the buckskin. Reaching his hide-out, the cowboy lawman saddled up hastily and spurred out into the open.

Sizing up the lay of the terrain, Raine saw that by heading northeast across the rolling sage hills he would be able to take a short cut to the road which Grace Spear had taken in the direction of her ranch. With luck he might be able to overtake her. Or, failing in that, he could cut her sign and follow her trail to her destination.

Topping a rock-strewn hogback north of Mexitex, Raine was startled to see a body of horsemen leave the town, spurring at top speed in the direction he was going. The riders, six in number, had left a corral behind the big Longhorn Saloon and were streaking northward, paralleling the road Grace had taken.

"Mebbe my nerves are gettin' spooky," Raine grunted, roweling his buckskin into a long lope, "but I wouldn't be surprised if them buscaderos ain't trailin' that girl, same as me."

Intersecting the road which followed a section line due north, Raine raked his pony's flanks with redoubled energy as he caught a glimpse of Grace Spear disappearing into the rolling hills a mile ahead of him. A smudge of dust drifting above the rim of a winding barranca further to the east showed Raine where the mysterious body of horsemen from Mexitex were riding at an angle calculated to cut off the girl.

Ten minutes later, Clay Raine's uneasy hunch was intensified as he rocketed over a chaparral-mottled ridge and sighted Grace in the valley below. She had reined up fifty yards this side of a motte of smoke-trees through which the road had been built, and Raine saw sunrays glinting on the .32 Colt which the Circle Spear cowgirl had drawn from holster.

"She scents trouble," Raine grunted, "and I don't see hide nor hair of them buckos from Mexitex."

Even as he spoke, a rattle of gunshots was wafted to Raine's cars. An instant later the lawman caught sight of the sextette of horsemen, spurring out of the smoke-trees.

Bullets were kicking up geysers of dust on all sides of the bayed cowgirl. The riders were fanning out to surround her, and even at three hundred yards' distance, Raine saw Grace Spear pouch her six-gun and throw up her hands.

"I'll be danged!" gasped Raine, spurring off the road into the shelter of a crooked draw which gouged the hillside below him. "Them jaspers are aimin' to kill that girl—or else kidnap her!"

CHAPTER 8

Thundering Guns

RAINE GIGGED HIS WINDED BUCKSKIN AT RECKLESS speed down the zigzag coulee, riding low over the pommel to prevent his approach being spotted by Grace Spear's attackers.

The draw's mouth opened out on the valley floor a hundred feet from the smoke-tree motte which had hidden the ambushers, and Clay Raine skidded the buckskin to a halt as loud voices reached his ears.

"Keep them flippers reachin', senorita!" a harsh voice rang out. "We know yuh're pizen with them popguns yuh're packin', so don't make no booger moves!"

Leaping from stirrups, Clay Raine burrowed his way through a hedge of spiny *tornillos*, drawing a Colt as he moved.

"Mescal Curtcliff!" Grace Spear cried shrilly. "What on earth is the meaning of this?"

Raine halted just inside the *tornillo* thicket, as he

came in sight of the drama being enacted on the road just ahead of him. Grace Spear had dismounted from her strawberry roan, and was keeping her hands at hatbrim height as the six riders from Mexitex circled about her, drawn guns winking in the morning sunlight.

A shaggy-bearded six-footer wearing goathair chaps and an anthill-crowned Mexican sombrero had swung out of stirrups and was approaching her. A six-gun jutted from one fist, and a coil of sisal reata was looped over an elbow.

"Yuh're comin' with us, gal!" snarled the man Grace had addressed as "Mescal" Curtcliff. "We don't mean yuh no harm, but yuh got to come along easy-like."

Hot blood rushed into Clay Raine's twisted countenance as he saw Curtcliff reach out to empty the girl's holsters, thrusting the light .32 Colts into the waistband of his chaps.

"But why?" he heard Grace demand frantically. "What do you want with me?"

Curtcliff shrugged, shaking out the loop of his lariat.

"Little girls shouldn't ask questions!" he chuckled venomously. "But I'll tell yuh this much. Yuh're expectin' Goldpan Rassmussen, yore uncle, ain't yuh?"

From his hiding place in the *tornillo* growth, Clay Raine saw the Circle Spear cowgirl blanch ash-white.

"Yes. Everyone in town knows that. But—"

Curtcliff laughed jarringly as he reached out to seize one of Grace's wrists and thrust it into the hondo loop of his lass'-rope.

"Well, my little filly, yore uncle's goin' to be packin' plenty of cash with him. Just about enough *dinero* I'd say, to pay off the ransom we're goin' to ask—"

Brrrang! A gunshot interrupted Mescal Curtcliff and a little puff of alkali dust lifted from the kidnaper's steeple-peaked sombrero. Curtcliff released his grip on the girl's hand and spun about, ducking instinctively.

His henchmen snatched at reins as their broncs shied violently before the concussion of sound.

"Who done that?" demanded Curtcliff, his eyes hot with rage as he stared about. "Somebody's gettin' all-fired careless with their hogleg!"

Curtcliff broke off as his shuttling eyes spotted a wisp of gunsmoke spiraling upward from a hedge of *tornillo,* at the mouth of a draw a short distance across the road.

"My next shot won't be so careless, busky!" Clay Raine sang out, crouching low in his ambush and earing back the hammer of his Colt. "Yuh'll catch a hot slug in the noggin if you and yore mangy *companeros* don't grab a cloud pronto!"

Grace Spear tore off the loop of reata from her arm and whirled to catch the trailing reins of her pony, as Mescal Curtcliff checked his gun-draw and half-heartedly raised his arms.

"Wise girl," Raine thought approvingly. "Got a head on her shoulders. Fixin' to get out of the line of fire."

Lifting his voice to a menacing shout, the deputy marshal called out from his brushy ambuscade:

"Tell yore gun-hung pards to cool their saddles, Curtcliff! Line up in a row an' start marchin' thisaway. Yuh're all under a plenty heavy drop!"

Grace Spear, not wasting time mounting, led her roan out through the circle of kidnapers, without one of them moving to prevent her escape.

One of the mounted men swung a boot out of stirrup, as if to dismount in obedience to their unseen ambusher's order—and then inferno broke loose.

Whipping a Colt from holster, the outlaw who had

been in the act of dismounting triggered a shot under his uplifted arm, sending a .44 slug ripping through the *tornillos* an inch above Raine's head. Ducking lower, Raine snapped gun-hammer, saw the treacherous outlaw jerk violently in saddle as a slug ripped through his chest. The six-gun dropped into the dust and the gunhawk reeled in stirrups as his horse commenced bucking.

The momentary diversion shielded Curtcliff from Raine's line of fire, and the shaggy-bearded kidnaper seized his opportunity. He vaulted into saddle.

"*Vamoose*!" shouted the outlaw, plastering himself Indian-style on the far side of his pony. "Hard tellin' how many 'gulchers we're buckin'!"

An oath of dismay ground through Raine's teeth as he saw the six horsemen seize reins and spur forward, in a maneuver which hid Grace Spear and her horse from Raine's view.

Holding his fire, not daring to shoot at the escaping killers for fear of hitting the girl, Raine groaned as he saw Mescal Curtcliff, invisible save for a hand gripping the saddle horn and one boot sole hooked over the cantle, gallop off into the tangled hills.

Scattering in all directions, Curtcliff's henchmen lined out for cover, three of them twisting in saddle to spray the mouth of the draw with a fusillade of bullets.

Grace had prudently withdrawn into the shelter of the smoke-trees. Herself unarmed, the plucky cowgirl had no way of backing her rescuer's play.

Already the outlaw sextette were out of gun range, but the man Raine had tallied with his only shot was clinging to the saddle-horn and leaving a bloody trail behind him. Like prairie dogs scuttling to cover before the soaring shadow of an eagle, Curtcliff and his men vanished into the maze of barrancas ringing the motte of smoke-trees.

Clay Raine thrust his smoking Colt into holster and skulked back into the draw, appearing a moment later astride his buckskin. Galloping over to the smoke-trees where Grace was mounting her roan, the deputy marshal rasped:

"We'd best hightail it, ma'am. Soon as Curtcliff and his riffraff pards get their wits together they may try to surround us."

Staring curiously at her benefactor, Grace Spear led the way out from under the blue-gray smoke trees, heading northward down the winding road.

"This way—my home ranch is just over the hill yonder!" she cried back over her shoulder, as Clay Raine galloped alongside her off stirrup. "They wouldn't dare chase us down there. Too many of my cowboys are there."

Cometing up the long slope ahead, Raine twisted about in saddle to scan their back trail. He saw no trace of Curtcliff or his five henchmen, but there would be no relaxing their getaway until they had reached the safety of the Circle Spear.

Topping the rise stirrup by stirrup, Clay Raine saw Grace's home spread in the valley below, the whitewashed ranchhouse and barns gleaming in the sunlight. With a born cowman's range savvy, Raine could not suppress a breath of admiration as they sped down the slope toward the ranch buildings.

The Circle Spear was a big spread, obviously. It was situated in a hairpin bend of Comanche Creek, a tributary of the Rio Grande which emptied into the larger river at a point west of Mexitex town.

Pitifully few cattle dotted the rolling rangeland beyond the creek—mute testimony to last year's rustling raid on the Circle Spear by the Black Wolf and his hellions. But the spread was still by far and away the prettiest layout Raine had ever seen in the Lone Star State. He could easily see why the avaricious Mexitex banker, Kimball Hitchcock, would want to foreclose on the Circle Spear.

With her chestnut hair bannering behind her, Grace Spear sped down into a poplar-bordered lane leading up to the rambling Spanish-type ranchhouse. She rode with the lithe ease of a girl born to stirrup and cantleboard, putting to shame many of the so-called rodeo queens Clay Raine had seen win top money at various Wild West shows in the past.

With dust clouding about them, the two fugitives reined up in front of the picket fence surrounding the spacious lawns which led up to the whitewashed adobe, red-tile-roofed Circle Spear ranchhouse.

CHAPTER 9

Hot Lead Destiny

NOT UNTIL THEY HAD TIED THEIR PONY'S REINS TO THE iron rings set in the masonry gate posts did Grace Spear turn to get a close look at the man who had been providentially on hand to save her from an ambush trap.

"I—I don't know how to thank you, Mr.—Mr.—"

"Clay Raine is the name, Miss Spear," the deputy marshal said.

Removing his flat-brimmed Stetson, he smiled down at the girl. In that moment, he would have sworn he had never seen a more beautiful girl in all his rovings.

"Oh! I remember seeing you at the bank this morning."

Devilish lights twinkled in Raine's granite-gray orbs.

"If I hadn't shaved off the beard I was wearin' yesterday, yuh'd remember havin' met me on a more personal basis before that, Miss Spear." The Texan chuckled mischievously. "At twilight yesterday, remember? Yuh thought I was yore Uncle Gid."

Grace Spear's eyes were hidden by the longest pair of lashes Raine had ever seen. Her bronzed skin was suffused with crimson as she looked up.

"Forgive me for teasin' yuh about that, miss," Raine said, his face suddenly grave. "After all, yuh're prob'ly wondering how in—I mean, how come I was on hand to help yuh slip Curtcliff's loop, back there."

The girl's face clouded over, crowding her embarrassment into the background.

"Yes," she said, puzzled. "I—I'm so mixed up by all the things that have happened that I . . . But come into the house, Mr. Raine. We can talk things over in there."

Grace led the way up a pebbled path, under an arched porch floored with Spanish tiling, and unlocked a gleaming teakwood door. Entering the Circle Spear living room, Raine saw a massive rock fireplace, some deep-piled rugs, and the reddish gleam of a magnificent grand piano in a far corner, draped with an exquisite Castillian shawl. The Spears had once been rich.

"I'm a United States deputy marshal, Miss Spear," Raine said, after they had seated themselves on a divan in front of the hearth. "I haven't got a badge to prove it, but thereby hangs a tale. Mebbe I better speak my piece first . . ."

In terse, clipped sentences, Clay Raine outlined the

circumstances of his being in Mexitex—his purchase of a small-tally spread over in New Mexico, his last business errand as a lawman which was taking him to Laredo to turn over his badge to his superiors.

Grace Spear's eyes widened with growing alarm as she listened to his brusque account of what had befallen him after she had mistaken him for her uncle, Gid Rassmussen. He wound up with a recital of digging his own grave in Tequila Canyon, south of the Rio Grande, and of having pursued the Black Wolf back to Mexitex before daylight that morning.

"The reason I've stuck around, Miss Spear," Raine concluded gravely, "is—well, lay it to my overbearin' curiosity. Helpin' a purty girl in distress, I guess yuh'd call it. It goes without sayin' that the Black Wolf is honin' to waylay this uncle of yores. Seems his men think that Gid Rassmussen will arrive in town astraddle a palomino similar to my cayuse, yuh reckon?"

Grace nodded. "I—I guess I talked too much, as women are notorious for doing," she admitted. "You see, Mr. Raine, I've never seen Uncle Gid—that is, since I was a baby. He wrote me saying I could recognize him by the palomino horse he would be riding, and by his whiskers. That's why—last night when you got to town, I—well—"

Clay Raine brushed aside her discomfiture by asking abruptly:

"Do yuh know what the Golden Spur is—or was?"

She stared back at him, more puzzled now.

"The Golden Spur?" she repeated. "I never heard of it. It might be Uncle Gid's name for his gold claim. I told you, didn't I, that he's a prospector? He did write me, though, that he had a large treasure in sight—

money enough to keep Kim Hitchcock from taking this ranch away from me. But he never said anything about a golden spur."

Raine did not mask his disappointment. Instinct told him that the "Golden Spur" was a vital clue behind the Black Wolf's determination to capture Gid Rassmussen. He had hoped that Grace Spear, the old prospector's own niece, might shed some light on the mystery. Now the meaning of the Golden Spur seemed more obscure than ever.

"Speaking of this banker feller, Hitchcock—is he crooked?"

Grace's nose wrinkled in disgust.

"Hitchcock isn't an outlaw, if that's what you mean. He's just an arrogant, domineering Shylock. Money is his god. Half the ranchers in Big Bend county feel the weight of Hitchcock's heel. He—he has had the gall to propose matrimony to me on several occasions." Her voice trailed off, as she shuddered.

Raine leaned forward earnestly.

"I heard yuh call the ringleader of them kidnapers by name," he said, changing the subject. "Who is this hombre Mescal Curtcliff, Miss Spear?"

Grace's mouth twisted in a bitter smile.

"Curtcliff owns the biggest saloon and gambling hall in Mexitex—the Longhorn. He's a no-good rascal, rotten to the core. He and my father, Colonel Spear, were bitter enemies for years. Once when Dad was sheriff of Big Bend County, in his younger days, he jailed Curtcliff for being riotous. Curtcliff always swore he'd get even. But I—I never thought he would stoop to wreaking his vengeance on a dead man's daughter."

Raine got to his feet, hitching his gun harness grimly.

"At last we've got something to sink our teeth into,"

he said. "Curtcliff would have masked up if he hadn't been so dead shore of kidnaping you this mornin'."

"He thought Uncle Gid would ransom me, and—"

Raine shook his head.

"I got a hunch Curtcliff was interested in somethin' more than a bounty for yore life," he said. "I got a bee buzzin' in my bonnet that tells me Curtcliff may be the Black Wolf's right-hand man. Or"—the possibility that occurred to Raine brought a note of awe to his voice—"Curtcliff might even *be* the Black Wolf!"

The Circle Spear cowgirl nodded soberly.

"It isn't illogical to assume that," she agreed. "Curtcliff,s saloon has always been a gathering place of hoodlums—a 'festering cesspool of lawless souls' my father used to call the Longhorn."

Raine strode toward the door, his jaw set in grim determination. At the threshold he turned to face the comely young owner of the Circle Spear.

"What are you going to do?" she asked anxiously, running up to him. "Where are you going? You mustn't go back to Mexitex now. Curtcliff and his badmen would drygulch you on the way to town. They're undoubtedly keeping a watch on the ranch, from the hills somewhere."

Raine colored as she gripped one of his hands between her own. He cleared his throat nervously.

"I'm not forgettin' I'm still one of Uncle Sam's badge-toters," he reminded. "There are two jobs ahead of me, Miss Spear. One of 'em is to visit the Longhorn Saloon and make *habla* with this Curtcliff hombre, when he gets back. If he *is* the Black Wolf, I aim to draw his fangs. Then there's the matter of yore uncle. Gid Rassmussen may get to town today and walk smack into the Black Wolf's gang, same as I did last night. I aim to make shore yore uncle pays off that Hitchcock jasper before anything happens to him."

Worry burned bright in the larkspur depths of Grace's eyes as she saw the dogged purpose in the Texan's outthrust jaw.

"Reckon I'll be dustin' along," he said. "Yore crew is on the spread, huh? I won't be leavin' yuh alone here?"

"No. A dozen men are within call. But I wish—"

"*Bueno*. I'll stop wastin' yore time—and mine."

As Raine opened the door, Grace Spear reached up impulsively, pulled his head down to hers, and kissed him.

"That one wasn't for Uncle Gid," she said, drawing back. "I—I think I know you too well to beg you not to go gunning for Mescal Curtcliff today. But I want to warn you, Clay Raine—he has plenty of paid gunmen working at his Longhorn Saloon."

Raine clamped on his Stetson and adjusted the chin cord.

"I reckon nothin' could stop me now," he said, and laughed boyishly. "Well—I'll be back, ma'am. Mebbe with yore Uncle Gid. At any rate, I aim to square accounts with that Curtcliff's nake for what happened to yuh this mornin'."

Grace Spear stood in the doorway, her heart too full for words as she saw the lathy rider stride down the walk, unloop the buckskin's reins, and swing lightly into stirrups.

A premonition that she would never see the swashbuckling young lawman again overpowered the girl, as she returned his wave of farewell and watched him gallop off down the poplar-bordered lane toward Mexitex—and a hot lead destiny.

CHAPTER 10

Interrupted Showdown

KEEPING AWAY FROM THE CIRCLE SPEAR WAGON ROAD and with an eye peeled for Curtcliff and his kidnaping hellions, Clay Raine arrived in Mexitex an hour later, without untoward incident.

Passing the Big Bend County jailhouse and sheriff's office, Raine debated for a moment whether he should introduce himself to the law of Mexitex town, and obtain reinforcements for the job he had laid out for himself.

Always a hard-headed realist, he knew the odds he would be bucking in badgering Mescal Curtcliff in his gunhawk-swarming den. It might easily prove a suicidal job for a lone man.

Finally, though, he decided against looking up the Mexitex sheriff.

"Bein' a stranger in these parts, I don't even know if the local sheriff can be trusted," he told himself, riding on past the jail. "For all I know, he might be wearin' the Black Wolf's collar."

Raine sought out a small livery barn on a back street, diagonally across from the private corral behind Curtcliff's Longhorn Saloon, from which the kidnapers had ridden that morning. Leaving the buckskin at the stable for grooming and graining, the deputy marshal headed for the main street, sizing up the horses he saw rolling in the dust and watering at Curtcliff's trough.

None of the saddle stock showed any signs of having been ridden recently, leading Raine to the conclusion that Mescal Curtcliff and his henchmen had not as yet returned to town.

Making his way to the Trail House, Raine accosted the restaurant man, Dud, who had served him breakfast that morning.

"Grace Spear's prospectin' uncle may show up today," he told the restaurant man. "If he does, tell him to inquire at the Longhorn Saloon about how to find the Circle Spear Ranch, will you?"

Dud nodded, eyeing the cowboy lawman quizzically.

"Reckon I can. But what's the matter with me tellin' this Rassmussen hombre where the ranch is my ownself? He's supposed to meet Grace at the Trail House she told me."

Raine frowned impatiently. "Miss Spear has changed her plans. She's gone back home, and I aim to ride back to the ranch with Rassmussen. I'll be waitin' over at the Longhorn bar until further notice. Got that straight?"

Dud nodded apologetically.

"Shore. Shore, cowboy. No offense intended."

" '*Sta bueno.*" Raine chuckled, his manner softening. "How about dishin' me up a man-sized dinner, huh?"

After he had eaten, Clay Raine lounged across the busy street to the Longhorn Saloon and shouldered through the batwings into the main barroom.

Curtcliff's establishment was an elaborate one, worthy of its reputation of being Mexitex's biggest and best. Though it was early afternoon, three mustached, white-aproned bartenders were on duty behind the long mahogany counter.

Crystal chandeliers hung from the ceiling beams, the floor had been freshly sawdusted by swampers, and in the gambling annex adjoining the barroom, Raine could hear the click of a roulette ball, and a faro croupier's droning voice.

After scanning the drinkers lining the brass rail, Raine headed for the gambling room, his eyes keeping a sharp watchout for a glimpse of Mescal Curtcliff.

A few minutes later he had bought chips in a poker game which was starting, at the invitation of a man he recognized as Kimball Hitchcock, the president of the Stockman's Bank. Evidently he was enjoying the long siesta Grace had mentioned that morning as being one of Hitchcock's habits.

"I know you got money, John Law," the banker chuckled. "We can use some of it."

Raine played interminable hands of stud and draw, his mind only half on the cards because he kept constant watch on the barroom, anticipating Curtcliff's return. In spite of his lack of concentration, his pile of chips grew until, at four o'clock, Kim Hitchcock was broke. He withdrew from the game to return to his banking duties.

At sundown, Raine cashed in his chips and returned to the Trail House to eat supper. As yet, he had seen no sign of the saloon-keeper who had attempted to kidnap Grace Spear that morning.

Dud, the restaurant man, reported that Gid Rassmussen had not as yet put in his appearance.

A sense of growing tension grew within Clay Raine as he returned to his vigil at the Longhorn. In the back of his mind was worry over the failure of Grace Spear's uncle to arrive in the cowtown. The possibility that Mescal Curtcliff had decided to lie in ambush on the stage-coach road flanking the Rio Grande, to capture and rob the old prospector directly, grew like an obsession within the lawman, making him wonder if he were on the right track or not.

After an indifferent session at chuckaluck and black-jack Raine bought back into the poker game which Kim

Hitchcock had reopened. Now his luck left him, and by seven o'clock Raine's winnings had dwindled to barely enough chips to cover his bets.

The hands of the fly-specked clock over the barroom door pointed to eight-thirty when Clay Raine saw the batwings fan open to admit Mescal Curtcliff. The shaggy-haired outlaw was unaccompanied by his kidnaping henchmen. Without pausing, Curtcliff crossed the barroom, ducked under the bar leaf, and entered a door marked "Private."

"Looks like you're cleaned, John Law," observed Hitchcock, thumb-spreading his cards to expose a full house which raked in the pot and the last cent of Raine's winnings.

"Sorry, but IOUs from strangers, even star-toters, are frowned on in our fair city."

Raine pushed back his chair and stood up, grinning ruefully.

"Never could play poker worth a hang," he answered. "But I'll be back pronto, gentlemen. Might hock my guns at the bar for enough to put me back in the game."

Trying to mask his inner excitement, secretly thankful that he had an excuse to leave the poker game, Clay Raine headed into the barroom. As he entered the smoke-clouded room he saw the door of Curtcliff's office open and the Longhorn Saloon boss entered, clad now in a bartender's apron.

Raine's heart slammed his ribs as he edged up to the bar, finding a place among the drinkers. Sooner or later, Mescal Curtcliff would spot him among the customers. And when he did, the beefy saloon-keeper might recognize him as the waddy in the gaudy rodeo shirt who had ridden off with Grace Spear following the ill-fated kidnap attempt on the Circle Spear road that morning.

In all probability, Mescal Curtcliff would go for his guns. If so, the show-down would be short and sweet, and Raine knew he would have to fog out of the Longhorn in a hurry, once he had dropped Curtcliff. Grace had warned him that the bewhiskered saloonman was sided by plenty of gun-hung bodyguards.

Another bartender took Raine's order for three fingers of Bourbon, straight. Raine surreptitiously loosened his Colts in holsters as he saw Curtcliff moving toward him along the bar, swapping small talk with his various customers.

Another ten seconds, and Grace Spear's kidnaper would be at arm's length. If Curtcliff didn't recognize him, Raine already knew what he would say, words that would be prelude to shoot-out:

"Still kidnapin' women for a pastime, senor?"

But Fate moved to forestall the imminent showdown. Glancing at the backbar mirror as he laid a silver cartwheel on the bar in payment for his drink, Raine saw the batwing doors open to admit a scrawny oldster with a goatlike beard.

The old fellow strode to the bar, pausing at arm's length from where Raine stood. Mescal Curtcliff arrived opposite the bar at the same instant, and smirked professionally behind his curly mat of beard as the old-timer leaned forward.

"Name yore poison, stranger!" boomed Curtcliff.

"I ain't drinkin' at the moment, thank ye," answered the old man. "My name's Gideon Rassmussen. They told me over at the Trail House that you fellers in the Longhorn hyar could tell me how to reach my niece's ranch. The Circle Spear."

CHAPTER 11

Fate Rides the Darkness

CLAY RAINE SHARED THE SAME SURPRISE THAT gripped Mescal Curtcliff, causing the saloon-keeper's jaw to sag and the color to drain from his swarthy *mestizo* skin.

Then, with a visible effort, the Longhorn Saloon owner regained his composure.

"Be glad to oblige yuh, Rassmussen," Curtcliff's aid affably. "You go past the Trail House, back toward El Paso, and take the first street to the right. It jines up with a road leadin' due north into the *brasada* country. Yuh foller that road four, five miles, and it'll run smack into the Circle Spear."

Gid Rassmussen passed a tired hand over his eyes. The oldster plainly showed the effects of a long, grueling ride, for his beard was thick with trail dust and the harsh lines of exhaustion lay deep on his seamy face.

"Thank ye, friend," the prospector said. "Before I go, would you mind tellin' me whar I could locate a jasper name of Latigo Fellen? He'd be about fifty-odd, I reckon."

Clay Raine fingered his untouched whisky glass, as he saw the two men lock glances. Did Curtcliff hesitate in answering?

"Fellen? Don't believe any man by that monicker lives in Big Bend county, Rassmussen. I've lived along this stretch of the Rio Grande, man and boy, for nigh onto forty years now. Never crossed trails with no Latigo Fellen, that I can recollect."

Raine saw an expression of keen disappointment in the rheumy eyes of Grace Spear's uncle. His warped shoulders seemed to droop under the impact of Curtcliff's disclosure.

"Thanks ag'in," he said wearily. "Ain't see'd this feller Latigo Fellen in thirty years, myself. I—I just heard recent that he was runnin' some sort o' business hyar in Mexitex. He may be dead, for all I know."

The prospector turned and headed for the door. Raine hesitated, in the act of following the old man. Rassmussen would head directly for the Circle Spear Ranch, no doubt. There would be plenty of time to overtake him, after Curtcliff was disposed of. The important thing now was to keep an eye on the saloon-keeper, for Curtcliff was the most dangerous man Rassmussen could meet up with now.

As the batwing doors fanned shut on the old man's departing figure, Clay Raine turned toward the back bar, bracing himself for the showdown which Rassmussen's inopportune arrival had momentarily postponed.

In the few seconds that had elapsed since Rassmussen had left the bar, Mescal Curtcliff had not been idle. Raine's jaw tightened as he saw the saloonman heading toward the door of his private office, whipping off his barkeeper's apron and hanging it on a wall hook as he passed.

Unnoticed by the other drinkers at the bar, Clay Raine left the brass rail and hurried along the counter to halt opposite Curtcliff's door, as the saloon owner vanished inside. Glancing around, Raine saw that Curtcliff's staff of bartenders were busy at the moment, serving customers at the far end of the bar.

Ducking under the counter leaf, Raine moved swiftly to the office door and gripped the knob. So quickly had he carried out his decision to follow Curtcliff that his presence behind the counter had escaped the notice of any of the saloon personnel.

Opening the door with his left hand, the deputy marshal shielded the gun draw with his right hand as he stepped quickly into Curtcliff's office and closed the door behind him.

"I got business with you, senor—"

Raine's clipped whisper trailed off, as he heard the slam of a door on the opposite wall of the office.

A coal-oil lamp burned low on a card-littered table in the center of the room, and its glare revealed that the office was empty. Clothing on a hall tree beside the back door was swaying indicating that Mescal Curtcliff had snatched a hat off the rack on his swift way through the office.

"He was shore in an all-fired hurry."

Raine stalked across the room and jerked open the rear door. Outside he saw the corrals and stable shed of the Longhorn Saloon, looming eerie in the Texas moonlight against the backdrop of hills to northward.

A thudding of boots in the office behind him arrested Clay Raine in the act of heading for the back porch steps. The muscles of his throat constricted with dismay as he realized that his entry into Curtcliff's office must have been noticed, bringing the saloon-keeper's gun-hung henchmen in swift pursuit.

A hand was twisting the doorknob at his back as Clay Raine vaulted the low railing of the back porch and dropped to the weeds below, swinging into a low crouch, guns drawn. Lampshine flashed over the corral fence as three burly gunmen hurried out of the office door. They headed down the porch steps at a run, without looking to right or left.

"Reckon they wasn't after me at all. Curtcliff must have slipped 'em the high sign to foller him."

Raine stood up as he saw the three men vanish into Curtcliff's stable at the far end of the corral. Cocking a .45, the deputy marshal hurried down the fence in pursuit. He heard low voices as he reached the stable door.

"It was Rassmussen, shore enough," Curtcliff was saying. "Interdooced hisself to me at the bar."

"That's what we come in to tell yuh, Chief!" another hoarse voice replied from the darkness of the stable. "We seen this whiskered old goat come out of the Longhorn and fork a palomino nag at the hitch-rack. We figgered mebbe yuh hadn't seen him."

Raine slipped into the blackness of the stable, groping his way along the wall to where he could hear the four men busily slapping saddles aboard horses.

He realized, now, why Curtcliff's three henchmen had not been chasing him, Raine, on their way through the private office. They must have entered the Longhorn barroom seconds after Raine had entered Curtcliff's office.

"We'll have better luck with the old codger than we did with the girl this mornin'," Raine heard Curtcliff's ay quickly. "Rassmussen won't be suspectin' trouble, an' he's purty well ganted anyway."

A barn door swung open at the opposite end of the stable, and Raine leaped forward as he saw the silhouetted figures of Curtcliff and his gunhawks leading horses through the door into an alley flanking the saloon.

Raine realized exactly the set-up that was shaping in the

night. "Mescal" Curtcliff was planning to ambush Gid Rassmussen on his way to Grace Spear's ranch!

The barn door swung shut, and Raine crashed headlong over a shovel under foot. He landed in a carpet of moldy straw and lay there tensely, wondering if the departing outlaws had heard anything.

He got his answer in a creak of stirrup leather and a swift thud of hoofbeats on the alley outside. Curtcliff and his men were heading north, away from the main street.

Cursing his luck, Raine wasted a precious minute groping his way through the maze of stalls to reach the door through which the owlhooters had gone. When he stepped out into the moonlight, it was to see the saloon-keeper and his bodyguards galloping northward down the side street toward the *brasada* hills.

Raine jabbed his gun into holster, indecision staying him for the moment.

It would be useless to run out to the main street and seek to prevent Gid Rassmussen from leaving Mexitex. By now the old man was probably on his way to the Circle Spear.

Remembering the buckskin he had stabled at a livery barn on the side street a block north of the Longhorn, Clay Raine set out at a dead run down the alley Curtcliff had followed toward the outskirts of town.

He found the barn deserted. Rather than waste time looking up the stable hostler, Raine hurried inside and saddled up the buckskin which had carried him to Tequila Canyon and back the night before. The hostler appeared as Raine was leading the buckskin out into the street. Raine thrust a greenback into the barn-tender's hand and swung into stirrups, heading at a dead run out into the north-bound alleyway.

Reaching the fringe of the cowtown, Raine swerved the buckskin westward until he came to the wagon road leading to Grace Spear's outfit. Gid Rassmussen had undoubtedly passed this way within the past few minutes. Curtcliff and his ambush crew had headed directly into the hills, no doubt intending to outflank the old prospector and lie in wait for him somewhere ahead.

The knowledge that he had let members of Grace Spear's would-be kidnaping bunch slip through his fingers back at the Longhorn stable put a hot rush of anger through Raine's body. Bent low over saddle-horn, he roweled the buckskin to the utmost speed of which it was capable.

"I'm plumb loco for not gettin' Palomar out of that Trail House stable, instead of ridin' this crowbait all the time!"

Topping the first of the series of cactus-dotted ridges which corrugated the terrain between the Rio Grande and the Circle Spear spread, Clay Raine sighted Gid Rassmussen a quarter of a mile ahead.

The old prospector was jogging along at a lope, forking a palomino which was a dead ringer for Raine's Palomar. Somewhere out in the moongilded hills to the east, Mescal Curtcliff and his night riders would be lurking.

Skyrocketing down the long slope. Raine was swiftly overtaking Grace's uncle. Rassmussen's palomino was obviously jaded after a hard day's ride. Within five minutes the cowboy lawman knew he would be able to warn the old prospector of the peril which lay ahead.

"Rassmussen!"

Clay Raine's yell echoed over the Texas sage hills, as he saw the prospector's pony subside into a trot, up the opposite slope of the moonlit valley.

Rassmussen heard the yell, and reined up. Thundering ever closer, Raine realized that the prospector might mistake him for an enemy, as he saw the old man lean over to snake a saddle carbine from the boot under his left *rosadero.*

Even as the old man got the Winchester into the clear and was levering a shell into the barrel, a stab of flame winked out of the chaparral further up the slope. The thunderous blast of a rifle smote Raine's eardrums.

A yell of dismay blew through the lawman's teeth as he saw Gideon Rassmussen drop his .30-30 and claw at his chest. Then, as his palomino started bucking wildly, Rassmussen's scrawny frame left the stirrups and catapulted soddenly into a prickly pear clump at the roadside.

Curtcliff s drygulcher had struck first!

CHAPTER 12

Surrounded by Doom

ONE MOMENT WAS ALL CLAY RAINE NEEDED, TO COME alive to his own danger, as he saw Curtcliff and his longriders emerge from the mesquites on the skyline of the ridge and head down the road with guns blazing.

The Mexitex saloonman was not shooting at Gid Rassmussen, for the prospector had not budged since landing soddenly in the cactus clump. No, Raine himself was their target, and slugs were already whining like wasps about his ears as he skidded his buckskin to a halt.

Caught on the open road, with the ridge crest behind him still within range of Curtcliff's guns, Raine knew that he stood a grave chance of playing out his string in this secluded, rocky valley cupped in the moon-drenched Texas hills.

Curtcliff s men were sharpshooters, as was testified by the fact that their first shot from ambush had bullet-dumped Rassmussen from saddle, either dead or dying.

Brrt! A steel-jacketed rifle slug caromed off Raine's saddle-horn, bending the heavy brass at an angle and rocking the swellfork pommel back against the lawman's groin like a blow of a fist.

With desperate haste, Clay Raine kicked boots free of stirrups and frog-dived to the ground. He picked himself up as rubble sprayed against him in a stinging fusillade, from bullets placed too close for comfort.

Riding at a dead gallop down the hillside, Curtcliff's gunmen were shooting like wizards. Once they reined up and had the advantage of a steadier aim, Raine knew how his chances stacked up against quadruple odds.

Palming a six-gun, yet knowing he was at a desperate disadvantage with a short-ranged Colt against the rifles which opposed him, Raine ducked low and headed for a nest of glacial boulders a few yards off the road. He vaulted a barbed-wire fence like a steeple-chaser and landed on hands and knees in scrubby buffalo grass.

Glancing over his shoulder, he saw that Curtcliff had reined up alongside the fallen prospector. But his three gunmen had fanned out to left and right and center, bearing down on the lawman with smoke founting from their rifle bores.

Miraculously, Raine fought his way through a blizzard of lead and dived into the sheltering boulders. He scrabbled his way behind a moss-dappled chunk of granite and drew both guns, cuffing off his Stetson and raising up into a crouch.

Just outside of .45 range, the gunman who had continued straight down the road had reined up. But Raine's peril would come from two different angles, as one horseman spurred up the ridge to the west, while the other circled wide toward the east.

Another minute would see Raine surrounded, with at least two of his adversaries gaining the advantage of high ground which would make his boulder-nest hideout useless.

He leaned against the boulder, panting like a landed trout. Off through the moonlight, he saw Mescal Curtcliff dismounting and striding up to Gid Rassmussen's sprawled form.

"Reckon the old-timer is done for," muttered Raine, the bitter flood of complete defeat surging through his veins. "The devil of a lot of good I did Rassmussen tonight."

Raine gripped his Colt .45s in sweating hands, inwardly fuming at the limitations of a six-gun's range. The beefy owlhooter who was blocking the road mid-way down the slope from the spot of Rassmussen's fall had dismounted and was leaning against a fence post, supporting his Winchester on it.

Obviously, this outlaw was stationed there to make sure that Raine did not leave the rock-nest where he had sought refuge.

The other two riders, meanwhile, were deploying up the two hillsides, taking their time in the knowledge that they were in perfect position to stalk their prey at leisure. The first rider who gained a position overlooking Raine's hide-out would smoke the lawman out of cover, or kill him in his tracks.

Sweat oozed from Raine's pores as he waited. Unable

to leave the rocks without drawing the gunman's fire, waiting was the only thing he could do. Yet each passing moment was like another nail hammered in his coffin.

Squinting through the moonlight, he saw Mescal Curtcliff grip Rassmussen by the ankles and drag the old man's inert body out of the prickly pear growth. Then, stretching the prospector across the wagon-wheel ruts of the road, the Longhorn Saloon owner squatted down and proceeded to unbuckle the long-shanked Chihuahua spurs from Rassmussen's boots.

As he watched, Clay Raine felt his veins turn to ice. There was something grimly familiar about what Curtcliff was doing now.

A knife-blade winked in the moonshine as the saloonman scraped at the metal rowels of Rassmussen's spurs. A moment later Curtcliff got to his feet, tossing one of the prospector's spurs to the ground and thrusting the other under the waistband of his pants.

"It's the spur we been waitin' for, *amigos*!" called Mescal, walking back to his horse. "Now to take care of the salty buckaroo who's been messin' into our business twice today."

Curtcliff s first enigmatical words brought shouts of triumph from the three owlhooters who were surrounding Clay Raine. Nor was Curtcliff's declaration sheer gibberish to the bayed lawman.

"It's that Golden Spur angle again," groaned the Texan. "Curtcliff done exactly the same thing to Rassmussen's hooks that the Black Wolf done to mine, over in Coyotero."

Raine wondered grimly if Curtcliff's pocketknife had a staghorn handle, with a pigeon-blood ruby set in it. Signs were pointing unerringly to the hunch Raine had spoken of to Grace Spear earlier in the day—that Mescal Curtcliff, the half-breed Mexitex saloon owner, could be one and the same as the Black Wolf, king of Rio Grande smugglers.

A shout came from the mounted outlaw who had gained the crest of the ridge west of Raine's hideout. Well out of range of the deputy's short-guns, the outlaw was dismounting, levering a cartridge into the Winchester's breech.

"I got that busky spotted, Chief!" came the outlaw's yell, piercingly clear in the Texas night. "Shall I cut loose on the son, or do you want to cash in his chips, just for luck?"

Curtcliff, back in saddle, spurred across the road and sent his mustang over the barbed-wire fence. Raine waited tensely, searching the eastern skyline for his third adversary, as he saw Curtcliff gig his pony up the ridge to join his henchman.

"We got all night to salivate that jigger, boys!" Curtcliff's houted. "Let the fun begin. We'll smoke that cowpoke out of them rocks quicker'n yuh could sling a cat by the tail!"

Brrang! From the backbone of the western ridge, Curtcliff's gunnie opened fire.

Raine ducked involuntarily, as a .30-30 slug traced a gray-blue smear across the rock inches from his face. Withdrawing hastily, the bayed lawman eared back the hammers of both six-guns, hoping that by crouching lower he might lure the stalking outlaws within range of the Colts.

Then, like a knell of doom from the ridge to his right, a second rifle started hammering its death song. Steel-jacketed slugs knocked granite dust over Raine's body.

Twisting, he saw the skylined figure of his second opponent, who had him in plain view.

It was a hopeless trap. To leave the shelter of the boulder nest and seek to catch the buckskin down on the road would invite sure death before he had taken a dozen strides.

To remain among the rocks was equally suicidal. Caught between cross-fires, at no time could he find a spot where he would be out of view of at least one of his attackers.

"Looks like this is where I cash in my chips," grunted the lawman. "It wouldn't be so bad, if I had a rifle myself. At least I could go out shootin'."

Then, from a totally unexpected quarter, succor came to the beleagured waddy. Up the road toward Grace Spear's ranch, another rifle started booming.

Risking a bullet, Clay Raine lifted his head above the rocks. What he saw was so fantastically impossible that he wondered if it were a figment conjured out of the witch-glow of the Texas moon.

Gid Rassmussen, instead of being dead as both Raine and Curtcliff had assumed, had left the road where the saloon-keeper had dragged him. Unnoticed by the outlaws, Rassmussen had crawled over to his waiting palomino and had retrieved the saddle carbine which he had dropped to the dust before the impact of the bullet that had dumped him from saddle.

Now, sprawled flat on the ground in the shadow of his palomino, Rassmussen was triggering the Winchester with grim precision.

A high-pitched yell of agony came from the outlaw who had stationed himself further down the road at the outset of the mêleé. Before the echoes of Rassmussen's shot had died out on the Texas landscape, Raine saw

Curtcliff's rifle-toter totter forward and jack-knife himself over the barbed wire fence.

"Jehosephat!" came the startled yell from the gunman who had opened fire on Raine from the eastern slope. "That old goat has come to life, Chief!"

Swinging his rifle barrel, steadying the Winchester with his elbows propped in the dirt of the road, Gid Rassmussen drew a rock-steady bead on Raine's attacker. The .30-30 bucked savagely against the prospector's shoulder, and at a hundred-yard range, Raine saw Rassmussen's target fling up his arms, then topple limply from saddle.

Gid Rassmussen, born and bred in the Western outlands, had prided himself since youth on his ability to bring down a soaring *zopilote* hawk without benefit of buckshot. He was putting his marksmanship to a grim test tonight.

Sorely wounded as he was, the fallen prospector swiveled about on the road as Curtcliff and his surviving partner opened fire from the skyline of the western ridge. A glad cry welled from Clay Raine's throat as he bounded to his feet and sprinted out of the rocks, to draw Curtcliff's fire away from Rassmussen.

Slugs were peppering the road on all sides of the fallen prospector. But the old man's Winchester bagged a target with his third shot to keep his record clean.

Curtcliff's mustang reared on its hind legs with a trumpet of pain, piling the saloonman in a backward somersault to the ground. Before Curtcliff could pick himself up, his mustang's legs buckled and the horse collapsed, blood guttering from the bullet wound under its mane. Intentionally or not, Rassmussen's third shot had put the ambusher afoot.

As Raine leaped over the barbed-wire fence and hurried out into the road to snatch the reins of his buckskin before the pony could bolt, he saw Curtcliff racing along the ridge toward his mounted companion.

The owlhooter reached down to catch his chief's extended hand. A moment later Curtcliff was scrambling up behind his partner's cantle.

"We got the spur—the devil with that whangleather galoot!" came Curtcliff's yell. "Get this nag over the ridge, Gregorio!"

Clay Raine was in saddle by the time the double-laden horse vanished over the ridge, followed by Gid Rassmussen's vengeful stream of lead.

Seconds later Raine was galloping past the corpse of Rassmussen's first victim, jack-knifed over the barbed-wire fence. Then he was leaping out of stirrups to lead his horse up to where Rassmussen had settled in a dead faint, his white beard jammed against the hot breech of the Winchester which had saved Raine's life.

Stooping, the deputy rolled the old man over on his back. He winced as he saw the spreading blood which stained Rassmussen's shirt front. There was a bullet-hole in the oldster's ribs, dangerously near the heart.

"Got to get him to a medico," Raine muttered. "He'll bleed to death where he lies, if I don't."

In that grim moment, Clay Raine made his decision. The nearest doctor would be in Mexitex, but his chances of getting the wounded prospector to the Rio Grande cowtown would be slim. Merely because Curtcliff and his surviving *compañero* had fled over the ridge top to escape Rassmussen's deadly fire, did not mean the villainous duo would not seek to waylay them en route to town.

"Grace Spear's place is closer. Reckon I'll get her

uncle home, then ride for a doc."

Raine lifted the unconscious man astride the palomino, roping his arms to the saddle-horn with a lariat coiled at the pommel. Then, recovering Rassmussen's hot-barreled Winchester from the road, the lawman mounted the buckskin and dallied Rassmussen's hackamore around the horn.

Into the Texas night Raine headed, keeping an eye out for a reappearance of the two outlaws who might be lurking somewhere behind the ridge.

CHAPTER 13

Rassmussen's Secret

GRACE SPEAR AND THREE OF HER CIRCLE SPEAR cowboys were at the ranchhouse when Clay Raine walked up the front path, stooped under the inert burden of the wounded prospector. It seemed a miracle to Raine that the old man was still clinging to life.

"Yeah, it's yore uncle, ma'am," Raine said bluntly, as the girl came down the veranda steps, her face chalk-white in the moonlight. "Curtcliff's bunch drygulched him on his way out from Mexitex."

Eager hands helped Raine carry the old man inside and to a bedroom, where Grace stripped back blankets and helped lay the old man down on clean sheets.

The first shock of her uncle's fate having passed, Grace Spear became calm and machinelike in her duties as a nurse. By the time Raine and one of the Circle Spear punchers had peeled off the old man's blood-stained shirt, the cowgirl arrived from the kitchen with a kettle of hot water and a quantity of bandage linen over one arm.

Another cowboy returned from the bunkhouse with a quart bottle of whisky, and as Grace swabbed her uncle's chest wound, they managed to get a swallow of the fiery liquor down Rassmussen's throat.

While they worked, silently, and with feverish haste to stem the flow of lifeblood from the oldster's brisket, Raine sketched briefly the details of the attack on Rassmussen.

"He's bad hit, but he more'n accounted for hisself," the tight-lipped deputy finished up. "Two of Curtcliff's gunnies and that strappin' mustang of his are coyote bait. Rassmussen made that rifle set up and talk."

Rassmussen's eyes flickered open then, the first sign of life they had observed. Staring about, the prospector's gaze sought out his lovely niece, and a smile touched the white lips under his straggly waterfall mutache.

"Looks like—I boogered up—things, darlin'," the old man whispered. "My palomino—went lame on me—up Fort Stockton way. Slowed me up—a couple of days."

Grace put a cool palm on her uncle's contorted brow.

"Don't talk, Uncle Gid!" she enjoined the wounded man gently. "Just rest, and try to sleep. We'll have you fit as a fiddle by morning."

Gid Rassmussen shook his head feebly against the pillow.

"No—playin' out my string—*muy rapido*," he said huskily. "I'm afeared—girl—they got—Golden Spur. Spur no use—without yuh find it ag'in. Then—yuh got—look up feller name of—Latigo Fellen. I figger he's in Mexitex. Mebbeso—under different monicker now."

Rassmussen's voice was a haunting singsong, and

Clay Raine figured the prospector was sliding into delirium.

"We know the busky who 'gulched yuh, old-timer," the lawman said gently. "We'll square accounts for yuh."

Rassmussen struggled to open his eyes. His palsied hands reached to touch Grace's, as the girl endeavored to place a bandage on his guttering chest wound.

"No use—tryin' to patch up—old sawdust bag—like me, sweetheart," whispered the prospector. "Just read—letter—I sent yuh. Just read—letter—I—"

A paroxysm of coughing seized the game old desert rat, and when it had spent itself, one of Grace Spear's punchers put his arms on the girl's shoulders and turned her gently away.

Clay Raine, his face a bitter mask in the lamplight, reached down to pull a blood-stained sheet over the still form on the bed.

Gideon Rassmussen, who had rubbed shoulders with danger for three-score years and more, had died with his boots on. . . .

Out in the Circle Spear living room half an hour later, Clay Raine found Grace recovered from her grief, and surrounded by her rock-eyed waddies. There were only three of them here on the ranch with her tonight, for the rest of the outfit were on the range, or in town. The men here had introduced themselves to Raine as "Windy" McHail, the Circle Spear foreman; "Toady" Peters, Grace's horse wrangler, and "Cookie" Turlock, the ranch cook. These three men, like others of the outfit, had remained after Colonel Chris Spear's murder, standing by their girl boss without regard to drawing pay.

“Just before yore uncle breathed his last,” Clay Raine said to Grace gently, “he said somethin’ about readin’ a letter. Yuh got any idea what he meant, Miss Spear? Or was he just ravin’?”

The cowgirl got to her feet, drying her eyes with a neck scarf.

“Uncle Gid was fully conscious,” she said. “He did send me a sealed letter, along with the one telling me he was coming to Mexitex to help me. I—I’ll get it for you.”

She was absent only a few minutes. When she returned to the group of sober-faced men in front of the fireplace, she was carrying an envelope. Without speaking, she handed it to Clay Raine.

Turning the missive over, the Texas lawman read the scrawled legend on its face:

To be opened only in case of my death.
Gideon “Goldpan” Rassmussen.

Glancing up inquiringly, Raine saw Grace Spear nod her permission to open it.

“I’ll read it out loud, seein’ as yore uncle would prob’ly want it that way,” Clay Raine said, straightening out the paper which was closely scrawled with Rassmussen’s shaky penmanship. “I got a hunch it’ll be danged important to all of us.”

He opened the letter, glancing down the sheet of paper. The letter read:

> I am in hopes that I’ll be telling you what this letter contains in person, Grace darling. But I’m pretty old and ganted up, and I don’t want to take any chances. So I’m getting my story down on paper.
>
> You asked me to try and save your dad’s ranch for you, seeing as how it’s pretty heavy in the red, and no

beef stock on the Circle Spear range to pay off any debts, seeing as how this Black Wolf ladrone has whittled down your herd.

Like I told you, Grace, I'll be glad to help. As you know, I'm only a hard-rock prospector. I've spent a lifetime hunting color from Montana to Nevada and all through Arizona and parts of Old Mexico. I ain't never struck it what you would call rich. I've kept myself in grub and chawing tobacco, and I bought Silky, the palomino who shares my existence. She's a fine mare, Grace, and I want you to have her when I'm gone.

But I think I'm on the trail of something which will see an end to your troubles, girl. Not a gold mine, in the exact sense of the word, but gold enough to clear the Circle Spear, and keep your old uncle in comfort the rest of his days.

It's a long story, how I come to be on the track of this here gold I'm telling you about, so I reckon I'd best go back to the beginning.

It's a long time back. Your mother was a little girl then—my sister, God bless her memory. I was teamed up with another young gold-hunter I met over in Californy—a strapping young hellion who called hisself Latigo Fellen. Fellen was a New England Yankee, and was an educated hombre.

I don't know if he got in trouble back home and had to go West to escape the law, or what. I prefer to think he just had adventure in his blood, and all young adventurers in those days was heading West, me among them.

Anyhow, Fellen and me struck it off *bueno* from the first. We were prospecting in the Sunblaze Mountains, over in the Texas Big Bend country, when a big norther blew up and the sandstorm was followed by a cloudburst. Fellen and me, we took to cover after our hosses drowned in a gulch. We crawled into a cave. When daylight come, I'm a loco leppie if we didn't find out that the cloudburst had done washed out a grave, down in the gulch where we was hunting for the carcasses of our hosses, and the burrow with our pack and grub on it.

This wasn't no ordinary grave. The skeleton that had been washed up was dressed in rusty armor, and there was a crest on the helmet, which Latigo Fellen said was a coat of arms of a proud Castillian family from old Spain.

Fellen, being an educated cuss, said he was certain sure this skeleton belonged to one of Coronado's conquistadores. I'm no whizz on history, but Fellen told me that this Coronado gent was an explorer, commissioned by the King of Spain to hunt for the fabled Seven Cities of Cibola, which folks them days believed existed, just like the Fountain of Youth.

Well, Coronado's expedition covered northern Mexico and got up into what later was America, as far as Kansas. They didn't find them Cities of Cibola, just the pueblos of the Zunis and the wigwams of the plains Injuns. This was around 1540 A.D.

Them conquistadores roamed far and wide. The hosses they straddled were the granddaddies of the wild mustangs that are grazing all over the frontier today. Hosses were not known in the New World before the Spaniards brought 'em over.

Clay Raine looked up. "Kinda beginnin' to read like a history lesson, huh?" he remarked.

"Go on," Grace said tensely, and the lawman did.

But I'm getting off the track. Fellen and me, we found a buckskin pouch buried with this here conquistador. Texas is purty dry, most times, and this pouch had not rotted with the ages. Inside it was some corroded doubloons, and a sheepskin parchment with a map on it and a lot of writing that didn't look much like the Mexican lingo I talked.

It was old-time Spanish, what Fellen said was archaic, whatever that is, but Fellen had gone to a big university back East, he claimed, and he translated it. It seems that this here Spaniard had been Coronado's treasurer, his responsibility being to take care of the Spanish dinero that Coronado had been give by the King to finance his expedition.

The feller whose grave we found had cached the treasure somewheres near a big river, which Fellen and me identified as the Rio Grande. The map was drawed to show this conquistador how to find his cache again. Natural, he wouldn't carry a chest of gold around with him, with the danger of Indian attack and all.

Well, anyhow, the key to the hiding place of that Spanish gold was not in that parchment. The missing clues that were *not* on the parchment were of a pair of spurs with solid gold rowels on them. Queer spurs they was, because the rowels was riveted so they wouldn't turn, for some reason which had to do with the unraveling of the gold chart.

You can imagine, Grace, how excited me and Latigo was when we found this skeleton in armor was wearing a pair of spurs with gold rowels that wouldn't turn. We knowed then and there that we wouldn't have to spend the rest of our lives hunting float ore or virgin placer. We'd locate this conquistador's cache, and split the contents of that treasure chest.

We flipped a coin to see who would carry the treasure chart, and Fellen won. We trusted each other, you understand, but just to make things doubly sure there wouldn't be a doublecross, we each took one of the Golden Spurs, without both of which the treasure map would be worthless.

We was half starved by the time we reached El Paso, and set about outfitting an expedition to locate this cache. We had figured out from the parchment that it was somewhere pretty close to the junction of Comanche Creek and the Rio Grande. In other words, Grace, maybe within sight of the town of Mexitex!

But bad luck hit us in El Paso. Fellen got drunk and talked too much, and the next day when I went down to the saloon where I had last seen Fellen, there wasn't hide nor hair of him to be found. I got suspicious that he had tried to doublecross me, but I felt ashamed of myself a day or so later when a bloated, fish-bitten corpse was lifted out of the Rio Grande. It wore Fellen's clothes, so I decided some Mex had knifed him and robbed him and dumped him into the Rio.

The other Golden Spur and the Spanish parchment was missing, and that was the biggest blow I ever took in my life, Grace. I knowed Coronado's treasure was lost for all time to come.

Well, years and years passed by, and I kept on with my prospecting. My sister married Christopher Spear, and pretty soon you come along, Grace. I visited you down in Mexitex when you was a baby, too far back for you to recollect, I reckon.

Then, only a month go, I run acrost an old crony of mine from the early days. This feller told me that he'd seen Latigo Fellen, in the flesh, down in Mexitex, Texas! He said as how Fellen had changed considerable, naturally, with the years. This loco old coot didn't find out, though, what business Fellen was in now, but he said that Fellen sure did live in Mexitex, and for all he knew, might have raised a family.

Again Raine glanced up. "I'm beginnin' to get an almighty strong hunch," he said grimly.

"So am I," Grace said, awe in her eyes. "Read on, Clay."

Right then I knew the truth, Grace. Fellen *had* doublecrossed me in El Paso. Knifed some poor hombre and dressed him in his clothes and dumped him in the Rio Grande, to fool me into thinking he was dead. Where all along, Fellen believed he could locate Coronado's treasure, even without the Golden Spur I had.

The way I figger it, Latigo Fellen may have spent years around Mexitex, trying to locate that gold cache. I got my doubts if he did, though, on account of the Golden Spur I still carried around with me, being the missing key to the whole shebang.

Well, I was all set to light a shuck for Mexitex and look up Fellen, and get that parchment and the other Golden Spur at gun's point, if need be, when here pops up your letter, Grace, telling me the bank is about to foreclose on your dad's mortgage. So that's how it stacks up, honey. I'm coming to Mexitex, and I'm going to cross trails with Latigo Fellen. It shouldn't take long to dig up that gold of Coronado's. As I say, it will more than pay off your Circle Spear debts, and there should be enough left over to restock your range with prime feeders. Looking back on it, Grace, it looks like it was intended for that Spanish treasure to be yours. If Fellen and me had found it, when we was young, it would have been spent by now.

I reckon that's my yarn, child. If you read this, it will be because I'm dead. Wherever I'm buried, don't be afraid to dig up my bones, and get the Golden Spur from my left foot. Once you got it, I know you got friends who'll see that Latigo Fellen ponies up the other spur and that treasure map.

Your loving uncle,
Gideon Rassmussen.

CHAPTER 14

Plans for Vengeance

HUSH THAT WAS A GELID SILENCE WAS IN THE CIRCLE Spear living room, as Clay Raine finished reading. Raine himself broke the spell.

"This letter clears up a lot of riddles, *amigos*," he said soberly. "This Latigo Fellen hombre got wise, somehow or other, that Gideon Rassmussen was headin' for Mexitex, and he guessed the reason back of his visit. Now I'm shore it was Fellen's men that captured me the other night, thinkin' I was yore uncle, Miss Spear. That's why I was packed over to Fellen's hideaway in Coyotero—because I got no doubt but what Fellen turns out to be the Black Wolf. That's why the Wolf took out his knife and whittled at my spur rowels—to see if they were gold."

Raine stiffened as he remembered that Mescal Curtcliff had stolen the old prospector's Golden Spur tonight. That being the case, then Curtcliff and "Latigo" Fellen and the Black Wolf would be one and the same man! When the two ex-partners had met in the Longhorn Saloon, Rassmussen had failed to recognize Curtcliff behind his beard, after the passage of so many years.

Raine got to his feet, adjusting his holstered Colts more snugly against his thighs. His brittle gaze darted over Grace Spear and her three Circle Spear hands.

"Cheer up, *amigos*!" The cowboy lawman grinned. "Things ain't so *malo*, after all. Curtcliff won't leave the country. We know he's got Rassmussen's spur. Ten to one, Curtcliff'll start huntin' that gold of Coronado's come daylight tomorrow. I don't see why that gold shouldn't change hands."

The Circle Spear foreman, "Windy" McHail, jerked a thumb toward the antique clock on the mantel. The hands stood at sharp midnight.

"That gold better had change hands and this very day!" clipped the ramrod. "Kim Hitchcock's due to ride out here at high noon, Grace. I wouldn't be surprised if that pot-bellied skunk wouldn't try to force yuh to move out, if we don't have the gold to meet his mortgage."

Grace met her foreman's gaze.

"If we could just be *sure* of that Spanish gold of uncle's," she said dubiously. "I know of one man in Mexitex who would loan me the money to cover Kim's mortgage."

"Windy" McHail's brows arched with surprise.

"Yuh do? Then what we got to worry about?"

Clay Raine saw the girl's wry smile.

"Charlie Engel, the county coroner, has offered to

help me out financially several times," she said. "But Mr. Engel is not a rich man. He would have to borrow the money himself, to loan it to me. I couldn't count on more than thirty days to pay Mr. Engel back. It would just be postponing the black day of judgment, because naturally Kim Hitchcock would be the only person in Big Bend County to whom I could turn for help."

McHail strode over to a wall cabinet, opened it, and took out a pair of shell belts and holstered six-guns. Buckling the gun harness about his paunchy midriff, the ranch foreman swung his gaze toward Clay Raine.

"What are we waitin' for, *amigos*?" he barked hoarsely. "Let's rattle our hocks over to Mexitex and find out where this Latigo Fellen hombre hangs out. We'll have the gold to back up Engel's loan, before the end of the week—I'll bet on it!"

Grace Spear shook her head dubiously.

"I—I couldn't ask Mr. Engel to advance me any money on such fantastic security as Coronado's treasure," she told her foreman. "We've never even heard of Latigo Fellen, 'Windy,' and I imagine we know every citizen in the county. Fellen may have moved away, or died. Besides, Uncle Gid wasn't even sure that Fellen hadn't discovered that Spanish gold, years ago."

Clay Raine, who had been an interested listener to the discussion between Grace Spear and her range boss, spoke up.

"Several facts point to yore bein' mistaken, ma'am," he said. "Mescal Curtcliff wantin' to get hold of that Golden Spur proves the treasure hasn't been discovered yet. Besides, I'll stake my last blue chip that Curtcliff will turn out to be Latigo Fellen, under another name."

McHail strode over to where Raine stood and rubbed

his hands together briskly.

" 'Tempus is fidgitin', as the schoolbooks say,' the foreman remarked. "What are we waitin' here for? You an' me have got to dab our loops on Curtcliff before sun-up, Raine."

The deputy marshal nodded agreement. He glanced toward the door of the bedroom where Gideon Rassmussen was stiffening in death, then back to Grace Spear.

"Speakin' of yore friend the coroner, ma'am," suggested Raine, "I reckon yuh better let 'Windy' an' me take yore uncle's body back to Mexitex with us. Charlie Engel is an undertaker, ain't he?"

The girl got to her feet, her eyes tragic in the guttering firelight.

"I'll ride to town with you," she said. "I—I can't sleep. And we can't—can't leave Uncle Gid here. Besides, Uncle Gid was murdered. I want to report that murder to Mr. Engel. We can have Mescal Curtcliff arrested and hanged for tonight's crime. I shan't be satisfied until Curtcliff pays for what he did—on the gallows."

McHail and Raine went into the bedroom and shrouded Rassmussen's corpse in a blanket. Meanwhile, Toady Peters, the horse wrangler, hurried out to the Circle Spear cavvy corral and returned with the foreman's line-back dun and a leggy steel-dust mare, to carry Rassmussen back to Mexitex for burial in the town's Boot Hill overlooking the Rio Grande.

Grace Spear was waiting at the front gate when Raine and the foreman led up the horse to which they roped Gid Rassmussen's blanket-shrouded form. She was holding her uncle's prize palomino, Silky, by the headstall.

"Uncle Gid wanted me to have this palomino," she said, with a catch of grief in her voice. "I—I think I'll ride this mare to town tonight. She seems to realize that her master is gone, somehow. I imagine she wants to be near him as long as possible."

Weighed down by their mutual grief, and the tragic mission on which they were embarking, the riders exchanged few words as they headed southward down the poplar-bordered lane, with Clay Raine trailing the steel-duster which carried Rassmussen's body.

When they reached the wagon road which snaked across the hills toward the Rio Grande, Raine spurred his buckskin closer to McHail's stirrup.

"We got to be on the watch-out for Curtcliff," the lawman reminded the foreman. "After Rassmussen scared him off, ridin' double with one of his pards, there's a chance Curtcliff headed for town to get men to back his play. We can't afford to run into a bushwhack trap, not with Miss Spear ridin' with us."

McHail spurred into the lead, a Remington .45-70 rifle cradled across his pommel. Grace Spear brought up the rear, and Clay Raine could hear the girl weeping softly from time to time, as she followed the horse bearing her uncle's corpse.

The horses shied as they reached the moonlit valley where the corpses of Rassmussen's owlhoot victims were sprawled. A pair of coyotes fled into the shadows as they passed the dead man dangling over the barbed wire fence.

Many thoughts churned through Raine's head as they continued on toward Mexitex. Though Rassmussen's detailed letter, covering the amazing, weird history of the Golden Spur and the treasure it would unlock, had cleared up several mysteries that had bothered Raine since his arrival in Mexitex town.

He had little doubt but what he and McHail could locate the missing Latigo Fellen. Assuming that Fellen had changed his name to Curtcliff, it was not unlikely that the man had heard of his old-time partner's coming visit to Mexitex. The fact that Grace Spear had spent two days in the cowtown awaiting her uncle's arrival, and had talked freely of the purpose of her vigil, would have ensured news of Rassmussen's visit reaching Curtcliff.

If Curtcliff had been in possession of the Golden Spur's duplicate throughout the years—and it was logical to assume that Fellen would not have destroyed his spur, or the Castillian parchment which gave the partial key to the location of a treasure lost for over three centuries—it was not stretching probabilities that Curtcliff could be fairly sure that Gideon Rassmussen, likewise, had kept the second Golden Spur down through the years.

If this was the case, Curtcliff had plenty of motive for lying in wait for Rassmussen. His attempted kidnaping of Grace Spear had been for the purpose of making sure that Rassmussen would turn over the Golden Spur to him, as ransom for the safe return of his niece.

Crowding the background of Clay Raine's thoughts was the grim matter of the mortgage deadline which the Mexitex banker, Kim Hitchcock, held over Grace Spear.

Only eleven hours away was the expiration of Christopher Spear's note, and with that zero hour, Kim Hitchcock would become the owner of the Circle Spear. Having overheard the banker's conversation with Grace the day before, Raine knew that Hitchcock had no intention of granting her an extension of time. The

Circle Spear, even without a steer on its vast range, was a prize for the cold-hearted Texas financier.

They arrived in Mexitex just as the moon was setting over the western skyline, and Raine breathed easier as he saw the cowtown in the offing. The brilliant moonlight had given them safe passage over the *brasada* hills from the Circle Spear, minimizing the peril of an ambush in case Mescal Curtcliff and his henchmen were abroad in the night.

Riding up the main street, Raine saw that the Longhorn Saloon was the only building in town whose windows were ablaze with lamplight. Raucous laughter came from the barroom, and from inside the gambling annex sounded the nasal singsong of the faro croupier, the clatter of the roulette wheel, the boisterous voices of men gathered around the craps table.

"This here's the coroner's office," grunted Windy McHail, drawing rein before a false-fronted shack with a sign which identified it as the Big Bend County Undertaking Parlors. "Engel won't be up, this time of night."

Grace Spear reined up between the two men.

"We can tie Uncle Gid's horse to the rack here," the girl said, in a voice which she struggled to keep calm. "You and I can walk over to Mr. Engel's cottage on Estecado Street, Windy, and wake him up. I—I want to report Uncle's murder as soon as possible."

The three riders tied their ponies to the undertaker's hitchrack, across the street from the Longhorn Saloon. Except for a couple of celebrants fast asleep in the muddy gutter in front of Curtcliff's place, the main street was deserted at this hour.

Grace Spear and her foreman started off by a side

street in the direction of the Rio Grande. Seeing that Clay Raine was not accompanying them, the cowgirl asked worriedly:

"What are you going to do, Clay?"

The deputy marshal jerked his head toward the saloon.

"I aim to see if Mescal Curtcliff is back yet."

Windy McHail scratched his double chins excitedly.

"If yuh're aimin' to have a showdown with that bushwhacker, I want to be cut in on the deal!" he cried.

"No," vetoed Raine. "You stick with Miss Spear, Windy. And while yuh're talkin' to Mr. Engel, ma'am, yuh might broach the possibility of borrowin' that money. I'm right shore we can cover Engel's loan within a week or so at the most."

Raine waited until McHail and his cowgirl boss had vanished down the side street on their way to the coroner's home. Then he turned and strode across the deserted street and through the slatted half-doors of Curtcliff's saloon.

Pausing inside the doorway, Raine saw that the Longhorn was still doing a rush business, though dawn was but three hours off. Drinkers lined the bar, keeping five bartenders busy sloshing out rotgut. Mescal Curtcliff was nowhere to be seen.

"Lookin' for somebody, hombre?"

Raine started, then turned to face a consumptive-looking swamper who was scattering fresh sawdust over the floor.

"Yeah. The boss. Curtcliff."

The swamper shook his head.

"Mescal ain't around tonight, cowboy. Yuh might find him over at his place in Coyotero—providin' the customs officers will let yuh across the international bridge this time o'night."

The swamper's words made Raine's heart thump.

"Yuh say Curtcliff owns another saloon? In Mexico?"

The swamper spat a brown gobbet of tobacco juice at a distant cuspidor, and nodded as he resumed sawdusting the floor.

"Yep. The *Tres Cruces Cantina,* over on Cinco del Mayo Street. Mescal divides his time between his two saloons."

Clay Raine walked back to the Longhorn porch, his brain awhirl.

Inexorably, the facts were pointing toward the confirmation of Raine's belief that Curtcliff and the Black Wolf were one and the same. For the Black Wolf's hide-out was in a Mexican saloon over in Coyotero. If Curtcliff owned a *cantina* on the Chihuahua side of the Rio, it could well be the same establishment in whose cellar Clay Raine had faced the smuggling king of the Rio Grande!

CHAPTER 15

Stolen Horse

JUST AS RAINE WAS IN THE ACT OF HEADING DOWN THE saloon steps, the batwing doors opened behind him and he glanced back to see Kim Hitchcock's familiar frock-coated figure leaving the barroom.

"Ah—my John Law friend!" boomed the president of the Stockman's Bank, pausing to light a Cuban cheroot. "I expected to see you across the poker table tonight, my friend. What's the matter? Couldn't raise any money on your six-guns?"

Raine's mouth compressed grimly as he returned the banker's cold stare.

"Speakin' of money, Hitchcock—today's the day yuh aim to take over Grace Spear's ranch, ain't it?"

Hitchcock halted in the act of turning down the sidewalk on his way home. He turned, his eyes narrowing as he surveyed the rangy lawman.

"For a tin-star who ain't been in town long, you know a lot, don't you?" sneered the bank president.

"I asked yuh a question, Hitchcock."

The ebb and flow of the coal on the cheroot between Hitchcock's teeth cast a satanic glow over the banker's malevolent visage.

"Off-hand, I'd say it was none of your business, John Law!" rejoined the financier. "But since you seem to know—yes. Colonel Spear's mortgage falls due at noon today."

Raine fished in his shirt pocket for makings.

"Yuh ain't foreclosin' on Grace's spread, Hitchcock," he said coolly. "Yuh're gettin' the money in full, this mornin'."

Hitchcock stiffened. He whirled the cigar across his gashlike, blade-thin lips.

"Yes?" he countered. "That means that Grace's uncle showed up with the *dinero,* then?"

Raine jerked a thumb across the street to where Gideon Rassmussen's corpse was lashed to a Circle Spear cowpony.

"Rassmussen was murdered tonight, Hitchcock. But the money will be on the barrel-head, just the same. I'll see to that."

Hitchcock's face turned a shade paler in the reflected glare of lamplight from the saloon windows. He seemed to be wrestling with inner thoughts, conflicting emotions. Finally he relaxed, and turned on his heel.

" *'Sta bueno,*" he called back. "Banking is my business—not cattle. If Grace can clear her debts to my bank, well and good. But if the money and interest isn't on hand by twelve o'clock noon, the Circle Spear becomes my property."

Clay Raine stood motionless, watching the tall banker stride off into the darkness. He heard Hitchcock's footsteps leave the board sidewalk and turn up a side street.

"Cold-blooded leech!" snarled the waddy, turning to go back to the horses. "He'd stab me in the back if he thought he could foreclose on Grace's ranch by puttin' me out of the way."

An instant later, Clay Raine came to a dead halt, staring goggle-eyed across the starlit expanse of the main street. Two men were leading Grace Spear's new palomino away from the hitch-rack in front of the undertaking parlors!

Raine's hand plummeted to gun butt as he headed swiftly across the street. The horse thieves were Mexicans, judging from the silhouetted outline of their cone-peaked sombreros and shrouding serapes.

The Mexicans had vanished down an alley between the coroner's shack and the Trail House, by the time Clay Raine reached the board walk. He was in the act of hurrying into the darkness after the two horse thieves when he heard a cautious voice call out from the distance, the sound magnified by the Trail House walls:

"*Andale,* Pablo! Have you got the girl's horse?"

"*Si*, senor."

Raine's jaw dropped on a shocked oath. The voice asking the question was Mescal Curtcliff's !

“I’ll be blowed!” whispered the lawman, moving swiftly to put the corner of the Trail House between him and the alley. “Those must be the Black Wolf’s men, chousing Grace’s pony.”

Then a new possibility occurred to Raine, a thought that brought ice-water filming from his pores.

Less than ten minutes ago, Grace and her cowboy foreman had been heading in the very direction from which Mescal Curtcliff’s voice had come. By some devilish mischance had the cowgirl and Windy McHail run afoul of the lawless saloon owner?

Pulses racing, Clay Raine hurried over to the coroner’s tie-rack. Gid Rassmussen’s corpse was still roped to the steel-ducter’s back. Windy McHail’s dun had not been disturbed, nor had the buckskin saddler Raine had been using since his arrival in Mexitex.

Trembling with anxiety, Raine untied the buckskin and swung into stirrups. Instead of heading down the alley where Curtcliff’s Mexicans had taken Rassmussen’s palomino mare, Raine swung out to circle the Trail House, on the far side of the livery stable where his own palomino, Palomar, was still bedded down.

Thinking back, Raine recalled something else which had escaped his notice at the time. Pablo, one of the horse thieves who had answered Curtcliff’s call from the darkness further down the alley, spoke with the voice of the Trail House stable hostler who had threatened to knife Raine two nights before!

Spurring the buckskin into a swift walk, Raine headed down the side street and reined sharp left across a vacant lot crowded with junk, broken wagons and other débris.

Distinctly to his ears came a mutter of Mexican

voices, somewhere ahead. Then he saw, indistinct in the wan starlight, three men leading Rassmussen's palomino down a side street toward the Rio Grande.

Leaving his horse in the shadow-clotted corridor between two weather-beaten shacks facing the back street, Raine hurried on foot through the darkness, at an angle calculated to come up behind Curtcliff and his henchmen. His eyes adjusting themselves to the darkness, the deputy marshal once more caught sight of Silky, the dead prospector's flaxen-tailed mare. The pony had been led up to a trim white cottage and tied to the bole of a flowering *jacaranda* tree in the front yard.

Raine's blood ran icy through his veins as he realized that Mescal Curtcliff had not been engaged in any mere theft of a fine horse tonight. More and more, Raine was coming to dread conclusion that Grace Spear and her foreman had run into trouble.

Ducking forward through the murk, Clay Raine paused as he gained the corner of the whitewashed picket-fence surrounding the cottage, before which Grace Spear's palomino had been taken. He dropped to a squatting position behind the pickets as he saw the cottage door open. Three men came out on the porch, two of them carrying a limp figure.

"Better tie her to the saddle-horn *compadres*!" came the hoarse voice of Mescal Curtcliff. "She's fainted colder'n a mackerel, and we can't take any chances of her fallin' out of the stirrups, while we're crossin' the Rio."

"*Si*, senor."

Despair hit Raine in the pit of the stomach like a blow from a mailed fist. Curtcliff's Mexicans were carrying Grace Spear's unconscious form under the *jacaranda* tree, preparing to load her aboard the palomino mare!

Leaping to his feet, Raine whipped both six-guns from holsters. His voice lashed the night like clanking sword-blades as he stalked down the side of the fence:

"Elevate, Curtcliff! Yuh ain't kidnapin' that girl while I—"

As if shot from a gun, Mescal Curtcliff whirled about at the sound of Raine's voice, then leaped like a panther for the cottage porch.

Spang! Raine's six-guns flashed in unison, bucking savagely against the crotch of his thumbs. But in the phantom starglow, the deputy marshal's aim was faulty. Slugs bit into the whitewashed clapboard of the house as Curtcliff kicked open the cottage door and vanished inside.

Pablo and his Mexican companion leaped toward the palomino as Raine swung his guns in their direction. Then the lawman held his fire, realizing that to risk a shot at the Mexican kidnapers would jeopardize the insensible cowgirl.

Red gun-flashes winked inside the cottage, as Mescal Curtcliff's guns blazed into action. Slivers ripped from the picket fence beside Clay Raine, and the deputy realized he was a prime target for the hidden marksman.

"Head for the Rio, men!" came Curtcliff's shout. "That buckaroo won't risk shootin' the girl—"

Desperation surged through Raine as he flung himself flat on the ground beside the fence. Standing up, he would be skylined, a perfect target for Mescal Curtcliff. Yet from where he lay he was helpless to prevent the Mexicans from making a getaway with Grace.

Crowding aside his own peril in that moment, nullifying the sense of outrage and impotence which welled up within him when he considered Curtcliff's daring reversal of the odds between them, a new sense, a stirring emotion that was utterly foreign to Raine's heart, took possession of him:

He realized with crushing finality, in that grim moment when he saw the Mexicans swinging Grace Spear's inert form aboard the waiting palomino, that he loved her! Nothing else mattered now but her safety!

CHAPTER 16

Midnight Chase

MESCAL CURTCLIFF HAD RESUMED HIS FIRE, SNIPING through the picket fence, questing for Raine's location. Dust and gravel stung the prostrate lawman on jaw and cheek. He wriggled about, thrusting a gun through the pickets and drawing a bead on the cottage door.

Then he held his trigger. A gun-flash now would betray his position, play right into Curtcliff's hands!

Hoofbeats thudded out from under the *jacaranda.* Raising his head, Clay Raine groaned as he saw one of the Mexicans holding Grace in saddle as he straddled the palomino's rump. The other Mexican was springing on foot in the direction of the cottage, rounding the corner of the yard.

A slug from Curtcliff's gun forced Raine to duck, as Grace's abductor forced the palomino to vault the low fence, his serape fluttering at his back.

Straight down the street in the direction of the Rio Grande the double-laden palomino sped, then veered to the right along a road which flanked the river bank, sparks flying from steel shoes.

"The dirty sons!"

Leaping to his feet, Clay Raine thumbed a bullet toward the black maw of the doorway where Mescal Curtcliff had forted up. He risked a slug in the back as he sprinted across the street, turning north toward the spot where he had left the buckskin.

Curtcliff's guns roared savagely behind him, but the slugs were wild as Raine zigzagged through the murk. Then bullets began to fall short as the sprinting lawman gained the alleyway between the buildings where his buckskin was waiting.

Swinging into saddle, Raine curveted the buckskin about and gouged the pony's flanks with steel.

Out into the open he sped, bent jockey-fashion over the buckskin's whipping mane. A rainstorm was brewing over the Sierra Caliente peaks on the Chihuahua side of the river, and a lightning flash stabbing across the heavens gave Clay Raine a glimpse of Grace Spear and her Mexican captor, streaking westward up the Rio Grande wagon road.

Once again Raine cursed the fact that he was not forking Palomar, as the slower-gaited buckskin faltered in its grueling pace toward the river bank road.

Raine remembered vaguely that a high barbed-wire fence flanked the Rio Grande as far as the limits of Mexitex. Grace's kidnaper would be unable to cross the Rio at any point barred by the international boundary line fence.

But Gid Rassmussen's palomino was swift and, double-laden though it was, Clay Raine doubted if he could overtake the Mexican kidnaper with the buckskin between his knees.

New peril threatened from the rear, as Raine hurtled out onto the Rio Grande road, through the dust of the palomino's flight. He hipped about in saddle, his lips compressing with alarm as he saw a rider heading his direction, from the cottage where Mescal Curtcliff had captured Grace Spear. The rider was coming like a thunderbolt, as if in pursuit.

Straining his eyes toward the darkness ahead, the cowboy lawman could make out the vague blur which was Grace and the Mexican. They had passed the end of the Mexitex fence, and were heading westward, following the Rio Grande upstream.

A rifle thundered behind Raine and his ear caught the high-pitched drone of a bullet overhead. Ducking instinctively, he glanced behind him, just as a second bolt of lightning slivered through the Mexican sky.

The greenish witch-light revealed that Raine's pursuer was Mescal Curtcliff. Apparently the outlaw had had a horse waiting, somewhere near the cottage.

Raine spurred on, oblivious to the threat of Curtcliff's rifle. As long as he could keep Grace's palomino in view, he would know where her kidnaper would cross the Rio. The palomino would be slowed down, swimming the muddy river toward the Chihuahua bank.

Then disaster struck!

Raine felt the buckskin under him jolt violently under an invisible impact of terrific force. The horse had been struck by a bullet. Raine sensed the truth, even before the whip-crack of Curtcliff's .30-30 reached his eardrums.

Lucky shot or no, the buckskin was finished. Collapsing at full gallop, the pony rammed its muzzle in the dirt, and Raine's instinctive movement of kicking his cowboots from stirrups saved his life.

Catapulting through space, Raine landed running, stumbled, sprawled headlong in the ruts. Then he bounced to his feet and leaped down the slope to his left into the dense tules and scrub willow which grew against the wire fence at the river's edge.

He dived into the protecting brush and had time to twist himself around and bring up his guns, as Mescal Curtcliff galloped past the sprawled carcass of the dead buckskin that blocked the road. The guns blazed in Raine's fist, but in the darkness it was impossible to hit the blurring target which the Mexitex saloonkeeper presented.

Without diminishing his horse's gait, Curtcliff flashed on by, his triumphant bellow reaching Raine's ears.

Lightning played along the Chihuahua peaks, giving Raine a glimpse of the saloonman as Curtcliff galloped out of Mexitex. The night hid Grace Spear and her kidnaper from view, somewhere to the westward.

A sense of overpowering futility mastered Clay Raine in that despairing moment. On foot, it would be impossible to trail the kidnapers, let alone overtake them. By now, the Mexican was probably taking Grace into the Rio Grande, making for the Chihuahua bank.

"Palomar!" gasped the deputy, remembering his own palomino. "I reckon there's no use leavin' him in that stable any longer."

Raine headed into the jumble of shacks which marked the outskirts of Mexitex, running toward the Trail House on the main street. He was vaguely aware that men were shouting in the night, over in the direction of the cottage where Grace had been taken away. The slam of gunfire was rousing the town.

Raine was panting with exhaustion by the time he reached the Trail House corral and ducked through the bars. A few moments later he was inside the stable, groping his way to Palomar's stall.

The palomino whickered delightedly as it caught its master's scent, felt Raine's caressing hand on his sleek neck as the lawman unsnapped the halter chain from the manger.

Leading Palomar out into the open, Raine struck a match and located his saddle, on the peg where he had seen it previously. With feverish haste he slapped the kak aboard the pony, jerked the latigo tight. He noted that his eleven-shot .30-30 repeater was still in the saddle-boot.

In the act of leading Palomar back toward the corral door, Clay Raine heard the front door of the livery barn being trundled open on its overhead rollers.

A gun leaped into Raine's palm as he saw the serape-clad figure of Pablo, the Mexican hostler, framed in the doorway. Pablo, then, had just returned to the barn after taking Grace Spear's palomino mare down to the cottage where Curtcliff waited.

"*Maños altos, cabrone*!"

The hostler froze in his tracks as Clay Raine's voice lashed out of the Stygian blackness of the stable. The lawman gave Pablo no chance to duck back outside. An instant later he was boring his gun barrel into the *mozo's* belly.

"I ain't got time to waste with yuh, *muchacho*!" snarled the Texican. "But I got some questions for yuh to answer, if yuh don't want a slug in yore middle . . . Where's Curtcliff takin' Grace Spear?"

Pablo's eyeballs rolled in stark horror.

"*Valgame,* senor—I do not now. I theenk he tak the senorita to the Black Wolf, *si*."

Raine laughed harshly, earing back the gunhammer to

full cock.

"Talk fast, *lechon!* Blast yore black heart, you know the Black Wolf is Mescal Curtcliff! Is he takin' her to the *Tres Cruces Cantina* over in Coyotera? Answer me!"

Genuine surprise flashed into Pablo's obsidian orbs.

"Senor Curtcliff ees the Black Wolf? By the sacred bones of Santa Sabatino, senor, I deed not know. The only time I see the Wolf, he wear the mask, *es verdad.*"

Pablo's arms were raised above his head, but as he felt Raine's pressure with the gun barrel lessen, his left hand came down and up, in a motion faster than a rattlesnake's strike. Raine saw the dull gleam of steel as the hostler, lashed to desperation, whipped a *cuchillo* from a hidden scabbard between his shoulder blades.

In the nick of time, Raine side-stepped the downward thrust of the razor-honed knife. Before the hostler could regain his balance for another stabbing blow, the American lawman smashed his gun barrel across Pablo's forehead.

Knocked cold, the hostler wilted in a heap at Raine's feet.

Jabbing the blood-smeared Colt into holster, Raine shoved the stable door open wider and whistled for Palomar. The magnificent stallion trotted outdoors, and Raine vaulted into saddle without bothering to close the stable door on the *mozo's* huddled form.

Men were running out of the Longhorn Saloon diagonally down the street, shouting to one another about the shooting they had heard a few moments before, as Raine sped westward out of Mexitex.

A few warm splashes of rain struck the lawman's face as he reined southward toward the Rio. It felt good to have Palomar under his saddle again. By comparison with the ill-fated buckskin he had been riding for the past two days, Palomar seemed to possess wings on all four hoofs.

Reaching the riverbank road, Raine saw a group of scantily-clad men swarming around the dead carcass of the buckskin, back at the edge of town.

The lawman smiled grimly as he sent Palomar streaking westward along the river bank. He snaked his Winchester from its boot under the *rosadero* and cranked a shell into the breech.

Mescal Curtcliff would face him on even terms, if their trails crossed again before this mad night was finished!

CHAPTER 17

South of the Border

BLACK THUNDERCLOUDS WERE ROLLING OVER THE menacing Chihuahua hills. Somewhere in the black depths of that beetling malpais, Grace Spear was riding to an unknown fate, this very minute.

Under what circumstances the cowgirl had met capture, Raine had not had time to contemplate upon. By some evil quirk of circumstance, she and her foreman must have blundered unexpectedly on Curtcliff. If Raine knew the caliber of Windy McHail, he doubted if the Circle Spear foreman had surrendered his boss without a fight.

More likely, Grace had seen her trusted foreman slain without warning. In all probability, disaster had struck inside the cottage, which Raine guessed was the home of Charlie Engel, the Mexitex coroner whom the girl had gone to see.

Two miles out of Mexitex, groping his way along the twisting riverbank road with the help of ever-increasing bursts of lightning, Clay Raine spotted fresh hoofprints leading off the road and toward the river, where the Rio Grande sluiced over a series of gravel bars. The tracks led to the water's edge, and on.

"This is where they took Grace south of the Border," Raine decided, spurring Palomar into the hock-deep stream. "Most likely this is where the Black Wolf's men took me across, too."

Reaching the Chihuahua bank, Raine located the fetlock-deep hoofprints in the muck where two horses had emerged from the Rio Grande. The tracks climbed the precipitous Mexican bank to a stock trail hugging the slope. They told the Texas deputy that Grace's palomino, and Mescal Curtcliff's mustang were heading eastward in the direction of Coyotero.

Raine gigged his own palomino up the declivity and reined to the left, his eyes scanning the terrain which was dissolving into a misty blur behind a veil of increasing rainfall.

He spurred forward in grim haste. The Texas norther which was ripping across the Rio Grande in a deluging assault on the Chihuahua wastelands would soon wipe out any trace of the kidnapers' trail.

Going got increasingly difficult, as the mud was turned to a gluey mire under hoof. At length Palomar was forced to a walk, and soon the mucky trail was a waterway, the downpour completely obliterating the tracks Raine was following.

Oblivious to the rain, forgetting the slicker thonged behind his cantle, Clay Raine pushed doggedly on, wet to the skin and with a slow, throbbing ache beginning to dig into his marrow.

Time and again the palomino stumbled under him. But the game pony sloshed on, cheating death every other minute where the crumbling trail followed precipitous rim-rocks.

Lightning flashes gave Raine occasional glimpses of the trail ahead. He saw no trace of Curtcliff or the Mexican who was abducting Grace Spear. But he drew comfort from the fact that the icy drizzle was shielding him from bushwhack bullets.

Finally the trail dipped down into a valley and Raine recognized the roofs of Coyotero below him, blurry and indistinct behind the rain whenever an electrical burst forked over the zenith. He sent Palomar skidding down the mucky hillside, until he had reached the wattle huts which fringed the edges of the Mexican settlement.

Occasional heavy chains of lightning gave him a view clear to the Texas side of the Rio, limning the buildings of Mexitex with an unearthly greenish glow. The tempest was rising in fury as Clay Raine reached the main street of Coyotero, the Cinco Del Mayo, which ended at the international bridge spanning the Rio Grande to Mexitex.

"All I got to go on is that Curtcliff must be takin' Grace to his saloon," Raine muttered, shivering as rain trickled down under his collar. "The swamper over at the Longhorn said as how Curtcliff's Mexican place was called the *Tres Cruces*."

A moment later Raine glimpsed the *cantina* he was hunting. A vivid lightning burst picked out a false-fronted adobe *cantina* on his right, with three crosses painted over its facade. This would be Curtcliff's

Mexican saloon, and in all probability the selfsame building where Raine himself had been taken, on the occasion of his meeting with the smuggler chief, Black Wolf.

Reining the palomino under the shelter of an arched arcade in front of a two-story *posada,* the cowboy lawman dismounted, hitching Palomar to an iron ring set in a pillar.

Out of the wet, he inspected his six-guns, twirling cylinders and checking the bore to make sure the rain had not put the .45s out of commission. Then he headed down the arcade, groping his way through dank gloom in the direction of the *Tres Cruces Cantina.*

Nearing the alley between *posada* and *cantina,* there came to Raine's ears the soggy slop-slop of a horse approaching the alley. Raine withdrew behind an archway pillar, hand on gun-butt. It was unlikely that any Coyoteren would be abroad in this weather. More probably the horseman was Mescal Curtcliff, who had skirted the Rio Grande by a safer, but longer trail, and therefore had arrived in town behind Raine.

A timely lightning-flash gave Raine a pinched-off picture of Cinco del Mayo Street then, and a close-up view of the rider who was spurring into the alley. His face was masked!

"The Black Wolf!" flashed to Raine. "That cinches it, Curtcliff *is* the Wolf. He must mask when he visits his Mexican place."

Raine squeezed his eyes shut, to retain the mental image he had of the Rio Grande smuggling boss. But there could be no mistaking that white mask made of a corn-meal sack.

The Texan stepped out from under the *posada* arcade, his boots slippery in ankle-deep mire. Lamplight was shafting from a window at the far end of the *Tres Cruces,* and its glare silhouetted the Black Wolf as he reined up in the window's light and dismounted.

Palming a six-pistol, Clay Raine hurried down the alley, keeping behind the miniature waterfall which swept off the *cantina's* tiled eaves.

Before he had covered half the distance down the saloon wall, he saw the Black Wolf's door-knock answered, and the outlaw went inside.

Raine's heart was pounding a rataplan on his ribs as he worked his way down the eaves gutter until he reached the doorstep.

On the other side of the door he made out the dull mutter of men's voices greeting the Black Wolf. But the din of raindrops on the corrugated iron roof of the *posada* next door prevented him from distinguishing individual voices.

He moved toward the window through which yellow lamplight poured out on the alley where the Black Wolf's mustang was huddled, tail to the wind, muzzle down. Then he drew back sharply, as a green window blind was jerked abruptly down to shut off the light.

Raine moved forward behind a jutting gunbarrel as he spotted a pin-hole in the shade where a pencil of light was spearing out, twinkling on the raindrops. Pushing his nose against the wet glass, Raine peered through the tear in the shade. But all he saw, from that angle, was the ceiling of the room inside—rough planks nailed to whitewashed beams.

"Ten to one that Mexican brought Grace in there," thought Raine, heading on toward the end of the building in search of another window. "They had enough head start to get here before Curtcliff did.

Reckon mebbe I ought to look around and see if I can spot where they stashed Rassmussen's palomino."

Rounding the end of the *Tres Cruces,* Raine flattened himself against the adobe wall as a lightning burst made night like day. But the wink of light revealed no window or door on that wall of the room where the Black Wolf had entered.

It did reveal an open hole in the low gable of the building, probably the door of a dove-cote, such as was frequently built into Mexican buildings. And Raine likewise saw a horizontal beam projecting out from the roof-tree, probably a continuation of the ridge pole which carpenters had not sawed off. He remembered this spot. The Black Wolf's cellar hideout was under this building.

Recalling that the ceiling of the interior room had wide cracks between its planking, Clay Raine got an idea. Swiftly he retraced his steps to the alley and approached the Black Wolf's horse.

Luck was with him. There was a coil of stout maguay fiber lass'-rope buckled to the smuggler's saddle pommel.

Seizing the Mexican *lazo* rope with a muttered prayer of thanksgiving, Raine hurried back behind the saloon. He shook out a loop in the wet reata, then backed away a few feet and waited for the next lightning flash to give him the location of the projecting roof beam overhead.

Twenty seconds later the heavens seemed to split open with electricity, a jagged seam of blinding light like a crack in a black Easter egg shell. Timing his upward cast of the rope with the ear-jolting thunder which followed the lightning burst, Raine sent his loop snaking upward.

His background of cowboy work served him well, for

his first throw was good. In the darkness, Raine pulled in the slack, felt the rope go taut in his grasp.

A few moments later Clay Raine was climbing hand over hand up the maguay rope, his boots getting toe holds on the interstices between the adobe bricks of the wall. Remote flickers of lightning on the Chihuahua peaks to the southward enabled him to spot the two-foot-square opening of the *palomera*.

Gripping the timber which silled the dove-cote door, Raine released the rope which dangled from the roof-tree pole, and climbed into the attic of the saloon's back room.

On hands and knees Raine crawled across the plank floor, through the cracks of which streamed lamplight from the room below. Stretched out on his belly, he shifted the position of his gun holsters to prevent the muzzles from scraping on the ceiling and betraying his presence in the attic.

Then he applied an eye to an inch-wide crack.

What Clay Raine saw jelled the blood in his arteries. He was looking straight down upon a table that was littered with whisky bottles, old papers and playing cards. But there was something else on the table—a faded yellow parchment covered with writing, weighted down at either end to keep it from rolling up.

And the objects which weighted down the vellum were a pair of spurs, the rowels of which glinted lemon-yellow under the rays of the lamp!

The Golden Spurs!

CHAPTER 18

Chihuahua Treasure-Hunt

EXCITEMENT STORMED THROUGH RAINE AS HE breathed those words softly. One of those spurs had belonged to Gideon Rassmussen, and was the spur which Curtcliff had stolen from the old prospector the night before. The other—was the companion spur which Rassmussen's old partner, Latigo Fellen, had preserved, along with the treasure-chart parchment which held the key to the location of Coronado's treasury!

Applying his ear to the crack, Raine could hear men talking.

"There's nothing to keep us from picking up that *oro* tomorrow, *amigos*," he heard one voice say. "The map tells me the cache is close to Coyotero—maybe within sight of town. All I've needed was Rassmussen's spur."

"But the spurs, senor!" cut in another voice, which Raine believed was the voice of Curtcliff's Mexican henchman, the peon who had kidnaped Grace Spear. "Why do you have to have these golden *espuelas,* senor?"

Raine could not be sure who answered the Mexican. The draining and guttering of rain down the tile roof immediately overhead made hearing difficult. But he had the impression that it was not Mescal Curtcliff who explained the importance of the Golden Spurs.

"According to this map, Gregorio," he could make out, "we have to lay these spurs on certain rocks, in hollows chiseled out for them. You notice the rowels do not revolve? It is because one point has been broken off each rowel. The direction that broken stub of rowel-point indicates gives us the direction of Coronado's gold-cache. *Sabe*?"

Rolling thunder obliterated Gregorio's reply.

Wriggling about, Raine once more peered through the ceiling crack. He had a bird's-eye view of the top of Gregorio's sopping *jipi*-straw sombrero, but from that angle he could not locate Curtcliff or the other man who had spoken.

Crawling from crack to crack, Raine endeavored to find a vantage point from which he could see if Grace were being held prisoner in the room below. But he could see nothing save the Navajo-rugged floor of the room, and the passing shadows of the men.

Raine smiled grimly. At least he had the advantage of surprise on his side. He could knock at the door from the alley, and when it was opened, get a drop on the man who opened it. His six-guns could do the talking for him, from then on. Curtcliff's Mexican *mozo* Gregorio, was certain to know Grace's whereabouts, if she were not in the room below. The wine-cellar under the saloon was a more likely prison.

He twisted about and crawled with infinite caution toward the opening in the gable. Rain gusted against his face as he reached out, groping for the lass'-rope.

Finding it, the deputy marshal swung his legs over the *palomera* sill and obtained a tight grip on the maguay, which was getting slippery from the rain. Then he swung out into space, intending to hand-over-hand his way to the ground twelve feet below.

An instinct of danger buzzed its rattles in the recesses of the lawman's brain as he started his descent of the dangling reata. And a lightning flash an instant later confirmed his premonition of peril.

Standing on the ground directly beneath him was a scrape-shrouded Mexican, staring at the coil of rope on the ground. Simultaneously with the burst of lightning, the *pelado's* gaze lifted upward, and Clay Raine saw an ugly pock-scarred face peering at him as he dangled in mid-air.

As the lightning winked off, Raine had a fleeting glimpse of the Mexican snatching a six-gun from under his serape.

Clay Raine's next action was reflex. There was no time to scramble back into the attic or to consider getting at one of his own guns.

Kicking both feet against the *cantina* wall, the Texican released the rope and leaped outward, plummeting downward toward the black shape of the Mexican who had discovered him.

In the blazing maw of the *pelado's* gun, Raine's body hurtled. Something like a hot iron seared his hip, and then Raine's spike heels smashed into the Mexican's upturned face.

The peon went down like a pole-axed steer under the terrific impact of a hundred and eighty pounds of bone and muscle crashing through ten feet of space. His sprawling form helped cushion the shock for Raine, as the deputy marshal rolled off into the mud.

Stunned by the impact, Clay Raine picked himself up groggily, then sank back to his knees. He was shaking his head dazedly, seeking to rid his brain of the cobwebs of pain which the jolt of landing had given him, when he saw the alley light up as the saloon door slammed open.

Men rushed out into the alley, yelling as they hurried out to investigate the shot.

Reflected light from the open door revealed Clay

Raine stumbling to his feet, revealed likewise the huddled figure of the Mexican, gun still in hand, who had been knocked cold as a fish by the man who had hurtled upon him like a ton of rocks.

Then guns blasted the night, as the Black Wolf in his flour-sack mask and his henchmen opened fire on the Texican.

Too dazed to risk shooting back, Clay Raine chose flight. Out of the zone of lamplight he fled, sprinting along the back end of the big *posada* next door to Curtcliff's place.

"The *Americano* who was saved by Senor Rassmussen!" came Gregorio's startled yell, thereby identifying the Mexican to Raine as the killer who had ridden off with Curtcliff after their ambush attack on Rassmussen. "He trailed us here, senores!"

Boots were slogging through the mud behind Raine as he headed up the opposite side of the *posada* and ducked into the arcade flanking Cinco del Mayo Street, where he had left his horse.

Raine had but one idea—to make his getaway, give his jarred senses time to assemble themselves. The bullet wound in his thigh was painful, but not crippling. Raine felt the warm wash of blood down his knee and calf, as he untied Palomar and scrambled into saddle.

As he reined out from under the *posada* arches into the Coyotero street, gunshots roared out from both sides of the Mexican hotel. The front doors of the *Tres Cruces Cantina* slammed open as Curtcliff's gun-hung *compadres* hurried out of the barroom to back their chief's play.

For Raine, there was but one avenue of escape—back toward the Rio Grande. He dared not risk losing himself in the maze of shacks on the outskirts of Coyotero, by heading for the hills. There was too much chance of being surrounded by the Black Wolf's men. Until he knew the extent of his leg wound, he had best play it safe—light a shuck for Texas.

Somewhere in the rain-lashed night behind him, Mexicans on horseback were lining out in swift pursuit. Clay Raine bent low over the pommel, spurring straight toward the international bridge which connected Coyotero with Mexitex, across the Rio Grande.

Past the Mexican border authorities' shack at the south end of the bridge, Raine sent his palomino hurtling. Yells resounded in his ears as sleepy Border guards tumbled out of their port of entry station.

Palomar's hoofs drummed over the plank bridge and through the half-light ahead of him Raine saw the locked gate of the U.S. Customs barring the Texas end of the bridge.

It was too late to halt the palomino on the slippery bridge. Raine rammed home the spurs and Palomar soared upwards, timing the leap with all the skill of a rodeo pony.

Steel-shod hoofs tore slivers from the top rail of the Customs gate. Then Palomar landed heavily on Texas soil, picked himself up without breaking stride, and shot past the American Border Patrol depot like a projectile from a cannon.

Alert Border guards rushed out into the rain, triggering revolvers at the horseman who had dared cross the international boundary at the port of entry. Lead was whistling about Raine's ears as he gave Palomar his head and reined leftward along the Rio Grande road.

The rain and the wind had cleared Raine's senses, now. He realized he might have to answer to the Border

Patrol for his seemingly illegal entry onto the American soil. But that would involve a lot of red tape, inasmuch as he did not have his Federal badge with him.

Then, through the darkness and pounding rain, Clay Raine spotted the familiar white cottage where Grace had been captured. He skidded Palomar into the back yard and flung himself from stirrups, leading the pony under the roof of a lean-to stable.

He was emerging from the shed when he saw the ghostly forms of horsemen flash past, heading west. It was unlikely that the Black Wolf had dared emulate Raine's feat in crashing the international gates. More probably, the riders were U.S. Border Patrolmen, who figured the lone horseman to be an exceptionally bold alien or smuggler.

Raine crossed to the front of the cottage, straddled the porch rail, and saw the open door from which Curtcliff had been shooting. The lawman hurried inside and closed the door. The cottage was as safe a place as any in which to hole-up until he had time to examine his leg wound.

Drawing blinds over the windows, Raine fumbled in his levis' pocket for a waterproof match-box made, in the frontier fashion, out of telescoped cartridge cases .45-70 and .44-40.

Scratching a match, Raine peered about the unfamiliar room. Then he drew in a breath of horror, as he saw two dead men sprawled on the living room rug.

One of them was the Circle Spear foreman, Windy McHail, whom Raine had last seen in the company of Grace Spear, heading for Coroner Charlie Engel's home. McHail had been shot in the forehead.

The other corpse was of a white-haired man clad in a

pair of blood-stained pajamas. It took little deduction to identify the dead man as the Big Bend County coroner, Engel. Before the match flickered out, Raine got the proof he needed that this cottage of doom belonged to the Mexitex undertaker, when he saw a pile of mail on a nearby table, the letters bearing Engel's name.

Tossing aside the dead match, Raine took stock of the situation. He had little difficulty in reconstructing events.

Engel had been roused from sleep by Grace and her foreman, who had come to report the murder of Gideon Rassmussen. The two Circle Spear people had been spotted en route to the cottage by Mescal Curtcliff.

Quite possibly the two men had been gunned down without warning, through the open window overlooking the porch. Curtcliff, getting the drop on Grace Spear, probably had dispatched his Mexican underling, Gregorio, to the main street to get the girl's pony. Pablo, the livery barn hostler, had assisted Gregorio. It all tied together.

"But why should Curtcliff want to kidnap the girl?" persisted the riddle in Clay Raine's mind. "He had the Golden Spur from Rassmussen. There couldn't have been any hope of getting ransom for Grace, unless Curtcliff figgered that bankin' hombre, Kim Hitchcock, might love her enough to buy her life."

Raine made his way to another room, and lighted a lamp. It was Charlie Engel's bedroom, judging from the tumbled blankets on the bed. The coroner had been summoned out of sleep to meet his doom, this night.

Peeling off his overalls, Clay Raine examined the bullet wound he had suffered in escaping from Curtcliff's saloon in Coyotero. As he had figured, it was a mere scratch, but it was bleeding freely.

Raine ripped a bandage from a bed sheet, stemmed the flow of blood, and bound the wound as best he could. Then he pulled on the wet levis and blew out the lamp.

"I can't waste time on this side of the Rio," he told himself, groping his way back to the living room and then outdoors. "Grace's life is at stake, if she hasn't already been killed. And I don't even know if she's bein' held prisoner at Curtcliff's place right now, or not!"

CHAPTER 19

Spanish Gold

DAWN WAS STAINING THE EASTERN SKYLINE, WITH ruddy promise, and Raine knew his only chance to leave Mexitex without being spotted by the Border officials, and detained for questioning, was to cross the Rio Grande in the darkness.

It would be risky to head westward for the ford across which he had trailed Curtcliff previously that night. Men would be blocking the trail west of Mexitex, perhaps returning from their futile chase.

Once more aboard Palomar, Raine headed north for the main street. Crossing it, he spotted the rain-lashed steel-dust gelding still hitched to the rack in front of Engel's undertaking parlors. No one as yet had discovered the corpse of Gideon Rassmussen roped to the Circle Spear horse.

Leaving town by the road which led to Grace's ranch, Raine doubled back into the *brasada* country, making a wide circuit of the Rio Grande cowtown.

Approaching dawn was thinning the night, giving Raine ample light to see the Rio Grande when he hit the river half a mile downstream from Mexitex. The cloudburst waters tumbling out of the Chihuahua uplands on the heels of the storm had turned the Rio into a muddy torrent, making ordinary fords impassable.

Taking his chances on being spotted by possible patrol riders, Raine wrapped up his rifle and six-guns inside his waterproof slicker and sent Palomar plunging into the river.

The palomino fought the rushing current, Raine guiding the pony through drifting logs and débris. He breathed easier when Palomar slogged his way up the Chihuahua bank.

A high, rock-studded ridge cut off Raine's view of the bottomlands where Coyotero had been built. The lawman headed inland until he was out of sight of the river, then spurred straight for the summit.

Sunrise blazed over the Mexican malpais just as Raine topped the foothill spur overlooking Coyotero from the southeast. But it was almost a false dawn, for scudding, slate-gray clouds held the sunrise to a pale duskiness.

Dismounting under the sheltering foliage of a *tepula* tree, Raine restored his Winchester to its scabbard under the saddle fender, and shrugged into his oilskin slicker. He was already wet to the skin, but the raincoat would turn the chill wind.

He kept a pair of binoculars strapped to his pommel. The Texan uncased the powerful glasses now, and focused them on the roofs of Coyotero.

Soon he had Mescal Curtcliff's rambling *Tres Cruces Cantina* under the circle of magnified vision. He swung the glasses to the left, studying the rear of the saloon.

The unconscious Mexican he had leaped upon in making his escape from the *cantina* attic had been removed, but the rope still dangled from the protruding ridge pole.

Suddenly Raine stiffened.

Three horsemen were emerging from a thatch-roofed barn in the rear of Curtcliff's place. The saffron oilskins they had donned against the fury of the rainstorm were exactly alike. But one of them was the Black Wolf. Raine knew that when his field-glasses picked out the eye-slitted white sack which served the smuggler boss as a mask.

Judging from the *jipi* straw headgear of one of his companions, Raine guessed that the Mexican kidnaper, Gregorio, also was one of the trio. Raine had no way of identifying the other rider.

Anxiously, the watching lawman waited for a fourth horse to emerge from the barn, hoping it would be the palomino mare, with Grace Spear riding it.

But no fourth horse appeared. The three riders vanished behind the barn, and a moment later reappeared, heading into the rugged Sierra Caliente foot-hills south of Coyotero.

"The Black Wolf's huntin' for Coronado's gold cache!" exclaimed the Texican, lowering the glasses. "I reckon I'll do a little scoutin' on that treasure hunt, myself!"

Raine figured out his plan of action, as he set off along the backbone of the foot-hill ridge. His best chance of learning the whereabouts of Grace Spear lay in capturing her abductor, Gregorio, and forcing the Mexican to talk under threat of death.

At the same time, by following the Black Wolf, he

would be in a position to force a show-down when the smuggler chief located the centuries-lost treasure of the conquistadores. He reasoned, as had others, that the cache was not far from Coyotero. That had been Rassmussen's idea, and Raine had heard one of the outlaws say the same, during the conference in Curtcliff's saloon.

"I reckon gold is gold, whether it's in brand-new nuggets or antique coins," Raine told himself. "Anyhow, I've got to get it for Grace, and I got plenty to do this mornin', if I'm to locate Grace and get her and the *dinero* to the Stockman's Bank before Hitchcock's mortgage deadline rolls around."

Half an hour later the rainfall diminished somewhat and Raine got his next glimpse of the three treasure-hunters. He saw them just as he was figuring on leaving the ridge and heading to a lower level to cut the Black Wolf's sign. To his alarm, the three slicker-clad outlaws were heading straight up the ridge toward him, as yet half a mile distant.

For a moment, Raine thought the outlaws had discovered him and had abandoned their mission long enough to ride up for a shoot-out. Then he saw the owlhoot trio rein up and dismount on a rocky spur of ground immediately below him.

Lifting his field-glasses, the deputy marshal focused on the outlaws once more. He saw the Black Wolf studying a rain-glistening object which appeared to be a sheet of paper. Then Raine realized that it was the Coronado parchment, which Gid Rassmussen and his treacherous partner, Latigo Fellen, had discovered thirty years before. Odd that their discovery had been made after a rainstorm similar to this one had washed up the skeleton of a Spanish conquistador.

The Black Wolf was gesticulating excitedly, after rolling up the parchment. He pointed to a nearby rock, a distinctive-looking chunk of bubble-pitted lava, rose-pink in color.

Peering sharply through the field-glasses, Raine saw the Black Wolf's slicker-clad, sombreroed henchmen approach the lava boulder and lay one of the Golden Spurs into a hollow of the rock. They moved it about, it seemed to Raine, in accordance with instructions which the Black Wolf translated from the Spanish parchment.

"That'll be Rassmussen's spur, I reckon," Raine told himself. "Fellen needed that clue to point to the boulder he would lay the second Golden Spur on. Without Rassmussen's spur, the whole treasure chart was useless to him."

The three outlaws took turns sighting up the hillside in the direction, evidently, which was pointed out by the missing point in the spur rowel. Then, their haste showing their excitement, the outlaw trio climbed aboard their horses and set off up the hill, at an oblique angle which would bring them to the summit, Raine figured, at a point two hundred yards south of the spot where Raine sat his horse.

"Looks like this is where I call for a show-down on them galoots," the cowboy lawman told his palomino. "I'm stashin' you in the chaparral, Palomar. I can carry out this job better on foot, I reckon."

Raine dismounted and led the flaxen-maned pony back into a copse of rain-dripping mesquites, where the horse would not be spotted by the Black Wolf and his men upon their arrival at the summit. Then Raine set off along the backbone of the ridge, heading toward a jutting upthrust of *tufa* cliffs which seemed to be the destination of the three treasure seekers.

The deputy marshal had secreted himself in a nest of weed-grown talus by the time the Black Wolf spurred his mustang to the skyline, less than a hundred feet away. At this close range, the hidden lawman got his first close glimpse of the Wolf's companions. One of them, as he had guessed, was the kidnaping Mexican, Gregorio. But the third man was Mescal Curtcliff!

"I'll be teetotally gol-darned!" whispered Raine, easing a six-gun out of holster. "Curtcliff *ain't* the Black Wolf, then! Which means that the Wolf must be that Latigo Fellen hombre, for shore—whoever he turns out to be!"

Less than fifty feet away from Clay Raine's hide-out in the talus, the three outlaws once again dismounted. They were babbling excitedly, their voices blurred by the patter of rain, as Curtcliff and Gregorio gathered about the smuggler chief, who was once more consulting the Spanish parchment.

"At the foot of the scarp, this map says!" came the Black Wolf's cry. "We are to lay the second Golden Spur on the flat top of a boulder shaped like an anvil, with the shank pointing due north."

Raine squatted lower in the talus as he saw the three outlaws hasten toward his hiding place. Looking about with feverish excitement, the masked Black Wolf suddenly pointed—to one huge, eroded boulder that resembled an anvil.

But Raine could see why Latigo Fellen, despite possible years of search, had been unable to locate that particular rock, with what information he had from the parchment. The second Golden Spur—the one which had been in Gideon Rassmussen's possession—was the key to the direction in which the anvil rock lay. Without

Rassmussen's spur, a man might scour the Chihuahua malpais for a generation, hunting it. It would be worse than locating a needle in the proverbial haystack.

Mescal Curtcliff came running forward, carrying Latigo Fellen's duplicate of the Golden Spur in his hand. Resting the spur on the flat top of the anvil-shaped boulder, Curtcliff's wung the rowel until its shank pointed toward the Rio Grande.

"That gold is as good as ours, *amigos*!" cried the Black Wolf, kneeling to squint along the top of the rowel. "The chart says the treasure chest is hidden five paces in front of the broken point of this rowel."

Raine felt his own heart racing with excitement, as the Black Wolf pointed at an angle toward the *tufa* cliffs' base. Then, with the end of their treasure hunt in sight, the outlaw trio rushed forward, to stare at the blank face of the rock wall.

"Mebbe—mebbe somebody's located it accidental, before us!" jabbered the black-whiskered Curtcliff. "I don't see where no *oro* could be hid."

But the Black Wolf was pulling a jack-knife from a pocket under his slicker—the staghorn-handled knife with the inset pigeon-blood ruby, which Raine could recall so vividly from his first meeting with the Rio Grande *contrabandisto*.

"No, it must be hidden in a niche dug out of this cliff!" the outlaw exclaimed. "*Tufa* is a strange rock, *amigos*. When dry, it is like stone. But it can be moistened, and it is a natural cement then. The conquistadores undoubtedly mortared up the cache with *tufa*, and when it dried, no one would know the cliff had been tampered with."

Consulting the parchment for the last time, the Black

Wolf seemed to be reading off archaic measurements. Then, kneeling at the foot of the cliff, the outlaw chief set to work hacking at the time-smoothed stone with the point of his knife-blade.

Raine got to his feet, guns sliding from holsters. The three outlaws, their backs to him, did not notice the American lawman as he crept out of the talus pile, thumbs ready on knurled gun-hammers.

A sudden yell from the Black Wolf made Raine clamp shut his jaw, in the act of giving his show-down order to the trio. The Wolf's knife was chiseling into *tufa* which was softer than the surrounding virgin rock.

Pawing at the cliff with delirious abandon, the three outlaws tore out clods of Nature's own mortar. Then they reared back, staring at the corroded brass handles of a small, rust-eaten casket which the Black Wolf had excavated from the niche carved from the cliff by the Toledo blades of Spanish explorers dead for nearly four hundred years.

"We're rich, *amigos*!" yelled the Black Wolf, his breath pushing out the fabric of his white mask. "This little chest is as heavy as if—"

The three outlaws knelt down, eyes glittering with fiendish greed as they saw the Black Wolf draw a long-barreled Colt. One thundering shot, and the rusty lock of the Spanish casket was smashed to bits.

Time seemed to stand still as the Black Wolf reached down with a trembling hand, to pry open the Coronado chest against the resistance of age-rusted hinges. And, revealed to the rain and the diffused sunlight, were tarnished gold coins. A fortune in ancient Spanish doubloons!

"Gold!" shrieked Mescal Curtcliff. "This is worth waitin' thirty years for, Chief!"

The triple click of two Colts coming to full cock reached the ears of the gold-lusting owlhooters, in that instant of transcendental triumph. Timed with the ominous sound came a low-pitched voice, deadly as a sidewinder's hiss:

"All right, *lechons!* The little party's over. Reach for the sky—pronto!"

CHAPTER 20

Behind the Wolf's Mask

UNNERVED, AND MOVING AS JERKILY AS MARIONETTES in a sideshow, the Black Wolf, Gregorio, and Mescal Curtcliff's tood up, with the opened gold chest at their feet.

They spun about—to face the deadly black bores of Marshal Clay Raine's jutting six-shooters, less than a dozen feet away.

"Yuh can shuck that mask, Latigo Fellen, as soon as youh've dropped that smokepole!" rasped the deputy marshal, edging forward with his gun-muzzles weaving like snakes' heads in front of the paralyzed trio. "The doublecross yuh pulled on Gid Rassmussen thirty years ago has come home to roost. It wasn't in the cards for you three buzzards to spend Coronado's money."

The Black Wolf dropped his six-gun into the mud. And then, without warning, the masked outlaw went berserk.

Leaping behind Mescal Curtcliff, the smuggler wrapped a steel-muscled arm about the saloonman's brisket, at the same time stooping to scoop up the gold chest, the act of a man given the strength of desperation, for the chest was heavy.

Hugging the casket against his ribs, the Black Wolf snatched a Colt from Curtcliff's holster and opened fire.

Bracing himself against the expected shock of tearing lead, Clay Raine triggered both guns. Slugs intended to smash the arm which the Black Wolf was using to hold Curtcliff as a living shield were a trifle low, and the saloon-keeper buckled under the shock of tunneling bullets.

Gregorio snapped out of his petrified trance then, pawing under his rain-sopped serape for a gun.

Dragging Curtcliff with him as protection against Raine's bullets, the Black Wolf headed for the waiting horses. The Wolf triggered Curtcliff's gun until it was empty, but the struggling saloonman was making the killer's aim go awry.

Faced by the closer menace of the Mexican's fire, Raine dropped to a crouch and swung his guns toward Gregorio. The two men fired in unison, but Gregorio's slugs ripped into the mud at Raine's feet.

Stumbling backward before the driving lead which Raine sent crashing into his chest and shoulder, Gregorio clung to life with miraculous persistence, fanning his spitting Colt with the heel of his left hand. And the *pelado's* game stand was giving the Black Wolf the precious seconds he needed.

Reaching his mustang, the Black Wolf released his bearlike hug on Curtcliff and leaped into saddle, balancing the Spanish treasure chest against the flat Brazos saddle-horn.

It took four bullets to drop Gregorio dead upon the pile of hacked-out *tufa*. But as Clay Raine whirled, he saw the Black Wolf spurring straight for the brink of the declivity.

Raine lunged forward, his gun-hammers clicking on empty cartridges as the Black Wolf risked all on a suicidal plunge down the roof-steep slope. An instant later the smuggler boss vanished over the lip of the ridge.

Mouthing oaths, Raine threw aside his empty guns, grabbed up the gun beside the dead Gregorio, and pounced toward Mescal Curtcliff. The saloonman was doubled up in agony at the spot where his traitorous *compadre* had dropped him, his life-blood painting the mud with crimson.

Stooping, Raine yanked the saloonman's remaining six-gun from holster. Rushing to the edge of the foot-hill slope, he saw that the Black Wolf was already out of Colt range. The killer's mustang was sledding on its haunches at a reckless clip down the muddy slope, toward an arroyo below, which Raine recognized as being none other than Tequila Canyon, where he had dug his grave.

A gagged cry from behind caused Raine to spin about. Mescal Curtcliff was dragging himself forward, his shaggy black beard smearing the mud.

"That—doublecrossin'—snake—didn't give—me a chance," choked the wounded outlaw, as Clay Raine knelt beside him. "I want—you to get my revenge—Texican—"

Raine stiffened warily as he saw Curtcliff roll over on his side and paw under his bloodied slicker. But it was not a derringer which Curtcliff fished from an inner pocket. It was a heavy iron key.

"This—key—liquor cellar—under my saloon—in Coyotero," wheezed the dying killer. "That cellar—where Grace Spear—prisoner. That's where—the

Wolf's headin'—with that gold—"

A pulse raced on Clay Raine's temple as he took the key from Curtcliff's lax fingers.

"Yore sand is runnin' out fast, buskie," rasped the Texan. "Tell me—who is the Wolf? Is he Latigo Fellen? Or are you Fellen?"

Curtcliff s eyes burned up into Raine's. The bullet-riddled saloonman was clinging to a spark of life which was fast ebbing.

"The Black Wolf—is Fellen—all right," gasped Curtcliff. "That's why—he had me—layin' for—Rassmussen hombre. The Wolf is—"

Curtcliff's head lurched, then slammed face down into the mud. A shudder racked his legs, then death stilled him.

Gripping the saloonman's key, Clay Raine got to his feet, new hope flooding through him. Gone was the necessity for trailing the Black Wolf through the trackless, rain-swept Mexican hills now. The Black Wolf would keep a rendezvous with destiny in his smuggler's headquarters under Curtcliff's dive.

"Yuh'll get yore vengeance, feller!" Raine told the dead outlaw, confessed partner of the Black Wolf's partner in crime in the lawless years past. "I'll do that favor for yuh, with relish!"

Flogging rain obscured the deputy marshal's return to Coyotero, when he arrived there, an hour later. He found the streets deserted, the Mexican populace forced indoors by the inclement weather.

Riding Palomar to the rear of the stable behind the *Tres Cruces Cantina,* Clay Raine ground-tied the pony and headed at a run across the mud-puddled back yard. He remembered, from his previous visit to Curtcliff's cellar, that its doorway was on the east wall, facing an alley.

He glanced about apprehensively as he headed toward the sloping door built against the foundation of the saloon. There was no way of telling whether the Black Wolf, heading for Coyotero by another route, had beaten him here or not.

Fitting the iron key into the cellar lock, Raine was relieved to see the big padlock snap open. Curtcliff had not doublecrossed him as his dying act, then.

Raine pulled open the door, letting rain splash down on the short flight of steps leading into the cellar. With determination he headed down the steps.

At the foot of the steps he halted stockstill, as he caught sight of Grace. The girl was conscious, but she was tied to an upright post supporting the barroom floor. A lamp flame guttered in the gust of wet air, from a wall sconce.

"Clay!" Grace cried out the name as she saw the cowboy lawman head across the floor.

And then, half-way to the girl's side Raine halted as he heard the door above the barroom steps creak open, to admit a momentary flash of lamplight from upstairs.

The door slammed shut, and heavy boots slogged down the steps. They came to a halt at the foot of the steps.

The Black Wolf, rain-wet mask, heavy slicker coat and all, stood stockstill on the cellar floor, his eyes flashing like a reptile's as he caught sight of Clay Raine.

Gold coins chinked inside the rust-eaten Spanish casket which the Black Wolf had been carrying under one arm, as the smuggler chief dropped the treasure chest and ripped aside his slicker tails to get at his remaining Colt.

"Don't force my hand, Fellen!" Raine shouted, one shoulder dropping in a gunslick's crouch. "I got yuh covered!"

Snarling as insanely as a bayed panther, the Black Wolf whipped out two Frontier Colts, brought one up spitting flame.

Grace Spear writhed against her ropes as she saw Clay Raine meet the outlaw's fire with return bullets, the gun he had taken from Mescal Curtcliff recoiling against his hand. In his other hand was Gregorio's gun.

A bullet hole appeared magically between the eye-slits in the Black Wolf's mask. Teetering forward like a hewn tree, the smuggler chief thudded to the floor, dead before he could pull trigger a second time.

Whipping a bowie knife from his belt, Clay Raine sprang forward and slashed the Circle Spear cowgirl's bonds asunder. She fell sobbing into his arms, but Raine pushed her aside for the moment as he raced across the saloon cellar to snatch up the gold-laden box of Spanish treasure, which would be Gideon Rassmussen's legacy to his niece.

Then before rejoining Grace, Raine stooped to hook the front sight of his smoking Colt under the hem of the Black Wolf's cornmeal-sack mask. With a sharp tug he stripped the disguise from the corpse's head. His eyes frogged out in stunned surprise, as he saw the smuggler king's contorted visage. The face of Latigo Fellen.

The jaw sagged open to reveal gold-capped teeth. Blood curtained the face from the bullet hole punched between his eyes. But even that scarlet mask did not hide his dual identity from Clay Raine. For it was also the face of Kimball Hitchcock, the banker!

Recovering himself, Raine raced back to seize Grace Spear's hand and drag her toward the alley door. He knew, now, why Grace had been kidnaped. Hitchcock would have given his prisoner the ghastly choice of marriage, or murder . . .

"We got to high-tail it before the barroom crowd comes down to see what the shootin's about, Grace!" Raine cried, as they headed for the spot where Palomar waited. "One thing we *won't* have to worry about is gettin' this box of gold to Hitchcock's bank in time to pay off that mortgage!"

Even with Palomar carrying double, it was not long before they were again in Texas. They entered the state by way of the international bridge, with Grace vouching for the man who rode behind the cantle of the saddle she occupied.

Reaching Mexitex, they paused briefly, to turn Gideon Rassmussen's corpse over to the local sheriff. Then they hurried on to the Circle Spear Ranch, to rest and talk things over. Their first chance to relax came inside the ranchhouse which Christopher Spear had bequeathed his daughter, in front of a cheery fireplace.

"Funny I didn't get wise to Hitchcock being the Black Wolf," the deputy marshal said musingly, as they watched the dancing flames. "Latigo Fellen changed his name to Hitchcock, after he'd give up tryin' to locate Coronado's gold with just one of yore uncle's spurs. Yuh remember Uncle Gid said as how Fellen was an educated Easterner? It was easy for Fellen—alias Kim Hitchcock—to establish himself in the bankin' business. And, as the Black Wolf, with men like Mescal Curtcliff workin' in his gang, he picked up a tidy bit of dinero on the side, maskin' his smugglin' work under the respectability of Mexitex's leadin' citizen."

After they had compared stories, and Grace had told

of her capture by Curtcliff in the home of Charlie Engel, Clay Raine got up his nerve to broach the topic nearest his heart.

"Yuh got a safe title to the Circle Spear now, but yuh'll need somebody to fill Windy McHail's shoes," he said, looking deep into her larkspur eyes. "I—I was on my way to Laredo to turn in my badge an' set up ranchin' for myself, Grace, when yuh rushed out and kissed me, and—and grounded my heart for keeps."

The cowgirl moved closer to him, until her head was against his shoulder.

"You mean you'd like to be the Circle Spear ramrod?" she asked. "Would you mind being paid off in Spanish doubloons?"

Clay Raine laughed, turning her face up to his.

"I got a herd of feeders over in New Mexico that would go a long way toward stockin' the Circle Spear," he said. "Course, I'd a whole lot rather yuh had a 'Mrs.' before yore name before them feeders was ready to ship to rail-head."

Cookie Turlock, the Circle Spear cook, entered the room at that moment, then withdrew in pop-eyed amazement so as not to interrupt his boss, who was locked in an embrace with the fastest-working waddy who had ever paid court to the belle of the Big Bend.

And it looked as if Cookie would be setting an extra plate at the ranch table, from here on out.

We hope that you enjoyed reading this
Sagebrush Large Print Western.
If you would like to read more Sagebrush titles,
ask your librarian or contact the Publishers:

United States and Canada

Thomas T. Beeler, *Publisher*
Post Office Box 659
Hampton Falls, New Hampshire 03844-0659
(800) 818-7574

**United Kingdom, Eire, and
the Republic of South Africa**

Isis Publishing Ltd
7 Centremead
Osney Mead
Oxford OX2 0ES England
(01865) 250333

Australia and New Zealand

Bolinda Publishing Pty Ltd
17 Mohr Street
Tullamarine, Victoria, 3043, Australia
1 800 335 364